Meadow Song

Beth E. Westcott

Scrivenings
PRESS
Quench your thirst for story.
www.ScriveningsPress.com

2020© Beth Westcott

Published by Scrivenings Press LLC
15 Lucky Lane
Morrilton, Arkansas 72110
https://ScriveningsPress.com

Printed in the United States of America

Paperback ISBN 978-1-64917-028-6
eBook ISBN 978-1-64917-029-3

Library of Congress Control Number: 2020940047

Cover by Diane Turpin, www.dianeturpindesigns.com

(Note: This book was previously published by Mantle Rock Publishing LLC and was re-published when MRP was acquired by Scrivenings Press LLC in 2020.)

All characters are fictional, and any resemblance to real people, either factional or historical, is purely coincidental.

Scripture taken from the New King James Version®. Copyright © 1982 by Thomas Nelson. Used by permission. All rights reserved.

Published in association with Jim Hart of Hartline Literary Agency, Pittsburgh, PA.

To my husband, Frank, who has stood with me for many years as I learned the craft of writing for publication. I love you.

To my mother, Rhoda Martin, who instilled in me a love of reading and is still an avid reader at 104.

PROLOGUE

"I'll get it!" Kate hurried to answer the front door of the home she shared with her parents.

She took a moment to smooth her skirt and check her hair in the hall mirror. It didn't matter that Tim was late. All day she'd been looking forward to a relaxing evening with him. This was their first dinner out in several weeks because they'd been so busy with work, wedding preparations, bridal showers, and marriage counseling. In three weeks they'd be married.

She opened the door, her smile fading. Sam Pratt, Tim's best friend, stood before her, grim and pale.

"Kate, I . . ." he stammered.

She peered over his shoulder. Rain shimmered in the light from the porch, but no Tim. Her heart in her throat, her stomach jittery, she whispered, "Come in." Floating in a cloud of unreality, she stepped back, allowing Sam to enter.

Her parents must have heard Sam's voice, because they suddenly stood behind her.

"Let's sit down in the living room," her dad suggested.

"Coffee?" her mother asked as they sat down. The young man shook his head.

Sam sat with his head down, resting it in his hands. Kate's chest tightened. Breathing became difficult. Her hands fisted in her lap.

He finally took a breath and looked at her, the expression in his eyes revealing the truth. "Kate, I'm sorry, there was an accident. Tim's gone."

CHAPTER ONE

*V*oices broke Kate's concentration. She squinted in the direction of the sound of a man and a child coming from the yard of the cute cottage up the road. The dark-haired young man looked vaguely familiar, but she didn't know why.

What a perfect day! Kate inhaled the scent that reminded her of picking wild strawberries as a child, of grass, and fresh air warmed by the sun. The sun in the sky behind her cast its rays over a sparkling meadow filled with butter-yellow buttercups, red columbine, and a profusion of other blooms, weaving patterns of color through the emerald green grass. A soft breeze stirred the branches of the blue spruce trees along the edge of the meadow and teased the loose strands of hair against Kate's cheek. Ellie had given her Tuesday afternoons off from Mill Valley Florist so she could paint. Tension and sorrow eased away with each brush stroke.

With a sigh, she turned back to her painting. Kate bit her lip as she studied the colors on her palette, mixing them to match the colors before her. She dabbed the brush in the blue-green tint before her, satisfied that the shade now on her brush was right for the trees. She leaned forward.

A young voice behind her said, "That's pretty. You're a good artist."

Kate jumped, nearly tipping over on her folding stool and barely holding on to her palette. Thankfully the brush avoided the painting as it slipped from Kate's fingers and fell to the ground, along with her straw hat. An angry comment died from her lips as she turned to look into a heart-shaped face with dark brown eyes, framed by chin-length brown hair. An air of fragility clung to the little girl in spite of sparkling eyes and rosy cheeks. Seeing her reminded Kate of her niece, and she suddenly longed for her family.

"Why, hello," Kate said, trying to cover up her fright by leaning over to pick up her hat. She placed it back on her head and plucked the grass-covered paintbrush from the ground with her thumb and forefinger. Finding a rag among her supplies, she wiped the grass from the brush and set it in a can of water.

The child's smile revealed a gap where two front teeth should be. She carefully examined Kate's painting. "It's so pretty. The colors are just right. Did you know the spruce trees sing when the wind blows through them?" She turned her gaze to the artist. "My name is Blythe. What's yours?"

The little girl's rushed words made Kate's mind spin. "I'm Kate. It's nice to meet you, Blythe. Are you lost?" The meadow, located a couple of miles from town, seemed a strange place for a child to be alone. Kate had noticed only a few houses on her way in.

"Oh, no, I live over there." The girl pointed to the cottage surrounded by flowers and a white picket fence. Painted white, with green trim, the small house reminded Kate of a storybook picture. She expected to see the Three Bears walk out at any moment. Smiling, she shook her head at her silly thoughts.

Blythe glanced over her shoulder and took a step closer to the easel to watch as Kate cleaned her brush and dipped it in the blue-green hue on her palette. She usually didn't allow anyone to watch while she worked, but the girl's interest and friendliness propelled her to lift the brush to the painting.

"Don't you think your father will be looking for you?"

The girl shook her head. "Oh, no. He's at work. Uncle Jack is taking care of me."

"Are you an artist? Do you like to paint?" Kate glanced toward the cottage. The man, probably Uncle Jack, stood by the fence, looking toward them. Maybe she should walk Blythe home.

Blythe nodded. "My mommy liked to paint, but she didn't do it as good as you. How do you do it? The daisies look so real." She raised her small hand and reached for the painted flowers.

"Don't touch it!" Kate yelled. The paintbrush slipped from her hand, landing in her lap. She grabbed the rag to blot the blue-green stain on her jeans.

The child's face fell, and she backed away, placing her hands behind her back. "I-I'm sorry." Tears stood in her eyes.

Kate took a deep breath and shook her head. "No, I'm sorry. I shouldn't have yelled at you. It's just that the paint is wet, and you would have smeared it."

"What would you do if the paint got smeared?" Blythe sniffed and wiped her eyes.

Kate quelled the urge to draw the girl into her arms and comfort her. Blythe was just curious when she reached for the daisies. Her loud outburst left her shaken. She cleaned the brush thoroughly with a rag and water. She dipped it in the paint again. "Well, I'm using acrylic paint, so I might be able to paint over—"

"Blythe! What are you doing, honey?" a harsh male voice called out.

Blythe waved. "I'm okay, Uncle Jack."

Kate looked up. Blythe's uncle Jack strode toward them. Dark hair, medium build, good-looking: Kate's mind scrambled to figure out where she had seen him before.

"How many times have you been told not to leave the yard or talk to strangers?" Kate recognized the concern that etched his voice. "I'm sorry she bothered you, miss."

Kate immediately saw the resemblance between Blythe and her uncle Jack, except he had blue eyes. Was that a glint of interest she saw in the uncle's eyes? It passed so quickly, she wasn't sure. Her interest in him, however, jolted her. She hadn't experienced this for a long time, not since Tim.

Self-conscious, she needed to explain her presence at the roadside by the meadow. "Really, she's no bother. I'm Kate Greenway. A friend recommended this place to me. It's beautiful here." Her nervous babbling made her blush.

The uncle's mouth turned up in a half-smile. He held out his hand to his niece. "Blythe, your doctor's appointment is in twenty minutes. We'll be late if we don't get going. I told you to wait in the yard."

"I'm sorry, Uncle Jack," she said, taking his hand. She pointed at the painting. "Isn't Kate's picture of the meadow pretty? She's an artist, like Mommy."

Jack briefly examined the painting and nodded. "Yes, it's nice." His eyes flickered to Kate's. "It was nice meeting you."

His blue gaze drew her in. "Nice to meet you too." She dragged her eyes back to the child. "Maybe I'll see you again, Blythe."

Kate watched as the two walked away, hand in hand. Blythe turned her head, smiled, and waved. Kate waved back. Placing the paintbrush in the can of water, she picked up her sketchbook, not wanting to lose the special quality of the little girl she had just met. On impulse, she sketched the uncle as well. As their car left the driveway, a lump formed in her throat and tears threatened. Loneliness enveloped her, blocking her previous joy. Homesickness washed over her, erasing the day's perfection. Memories of the tightness of her father's hug and the worry in her mother's eyes as she left Mountain View almost a year ago made the tears spill over and run down her cheeks. A cloud covered the sun, and she shivered in the breeze.

She wrapped her arms around her middle. On Sunday she should be celebrating her first wedding anniversary with Tim, if the drunk driver hadn't stolen Tim's life on that rainy evening a year ago. The drunk driver was sentenced to prison, but that didn't bring Tim back. Her self-imposed exile in Millvale helped her escape painful reminders, not the memories.

Perhaps treating herself to a meal at Mill Pond Diner would lift her spirits.

Kate carefully packed up her supplies and put them in the trunk of her car. She laid the painting on the back seat to keep it from being smudged. Taking one more look at the meadow and at the cottage, she laughed at her sudden notion to knock on the cottage door and ask for the Three Bears. She would be back. Perhaps she would meet the occupants of the cottage another time.

IN THE EARLY EVENING DOWNPOUR, Kate emerged from her car and ran into the diner. She shivered as she stepped into the air-conditioned building with its clean, shiny, red and chrome décor. She hung her rain-dampened, teal windbreaker on the back of a chair, wiped water drops from her hair, and dried her hands on her jeans. As she sat, the smell of food made her stomach growl.

"Thank you, Hannah." She accepted a menu from the teenage waitress. "Will you bring me a cup of hot tea, please?"

Hannah smiled. "Yes, ma'am, I'll be right back."

She tracked Hannah's light, quick movements as the teen greeted customers and laughed at a comment. Kate had been young like Hannah once, a long time ago. She sighed and opened the menu. As she considered her food choices, Kate fought homesickness for the second time that day. She blinked back tears. Hot soup and a salad would fit her budget and help chase away the chill. Hannah returned with the tea and took her order. After she left, Kate watched the raindrops make watery patterns on the window beside her, heard the muffled chatter of voices around her.

Suddenly a voice piped up. "Look, Uncle Jack. There's Kate."

Across the way, Blythe and her uncle sat in a booth. Blythe waved to her before leaning over to whisper something in Jack's ear. Several diners looked up. Kate stirred her tea, her cheeks hot, and pretended not to notice when Jack got up. But he was hard to ignore as he strolled toward her.

"Hi, I'm Jack Chambers, Blythe's uncle. We sort of met before." Kate looked up into intense blue eyes. Jack stuffed his fingers into his jeans pockets. "Blythe thought you looked lonely and would like to have you sit with us. Care to?" When she hesitated, he added, "Unless you're meeting someone."

Kate almost refused, but when she saw the expectant look on Blythe's face, she changed her mind. The girl's hopeful expression and the invitation offered a respite from her loneliness. "That would be nice. Thank you."

"No problem," he said with a shrug and a smile that made Kate's breath catch.

She hung her windbreaker over her arm and picked up the cup of tea. She didn't see Hannah, but she decided the waitress would find her.

"Sit here, Kate." Blythe patted the red, vinyl seat. Placing her cup of tea on the table, Kate slid into the booth next to the little girl. "Oh, goody!" To Kate's surprise, the girl snuggled up against her.

The ease of being with these new acquaintances also surprised Kate. The chatter and laughter flowed easily while they waited for their food.

"We like to eat here," she said. "Sometimes my daddy

comes, and we feed the ducks." Before Kate could comment about the ducks, Blythe continued. "I have three names." She counted them out on her fingers. "Blythe Amber Chambers. My daddy is Mark Chambers, and Uncle Jack is Jack Chambers."

Jack reached across the table to tweak a lock of his niece's hair. She grinned at him.

"Mark is my older brother," he explained, "and I help him take care of this little pixie."

Kate started to ask about Blythe's mother, but Hannah arrived with their food. She set down their dishes and smiled. "Enjoy your meal."

"Can I pray, Uncle Jack?"

With a nod, he replied, "Of course, Princess."

Blythe took Kate's hand and then Jack's. She waited, raising her eyebrows in their direction. Kate realized she expected all of them to hold hands as they prayed. Glancing at Jack, Kate rested her open hand on the table. He met her eyes and took her hand. A tingle ran up her arm at his touch. Did Jack feel it too? She closed her eyes.

The little girl prayed, "Dear God, Thank You for our food. Thank You for my new friend, Kate, and that she can eat with us. She's a good artist. Thank You that Uncle Jack takes care of me, and please keep my daddy safe. In Jesus' name, amen."

Touched by the child's prayer, Kate sat for a moment with her eyes downcast. Her now empty hands felt cold, her cheeks warm. When she looked up, Blythe was already munching on a French fry. Jack avoided eye contact with her, so she took a forkful of salad. A drip of dressing dribbled down her chin. She reached for the napkin on her lap and knocked it to the floor. As she bent to retrieve it, she rested her left hand on the table. Blythe pointed toward Kate's hand. "That's a pretty ring. My mommy had one like it."

Kate fingered the diamond ring, Tim's ring, which she still wore.

"Oh?" Jack leaned forward slightly to look. "Are you engaged?" He moved back and fidgeted with his iced tea glass.

"No, not really. I mean, I was." Kate's voice wobbled as she spoke. "But he died." She seldom talked about Tim, and she was uncomfortable revealing even this small part of her personal life to strangers. In Millvale, only Ellie and Ben, Pastor Clary, and Mrs. Matthews knew her story. Her lips trembled.

"I'm sorry," he said. "That must have been tough." His finger traced a pattern on the table top. "What happened?" She didn't answer immediately. He glanced up. "Or would you rather not talk about it?"

Kate twisted her ring, took a deep breath, and pressed her lips together. She struggled to control her emotions as memories washed over her. Jack's expression indicated sincere concern. Blythe sat watching her, not moving. "No. It's okay. Tim and I planned to be married a year ago. But just before the wedding, he was killed by a drunk driver." Kate sniffed and wiped tears from her face with her napkin.

"I'm sorry," he said. He slid his hand across the table toward hers but jerked it back to his lap.

Kate lifted her eyes from his hand to his face. "Taking off the ring would have been so final, I just kept wearing it." She clasped her hands together on her lap.

"Oh." Jack sat back and bit his lip. He shook his head slightly and frowned.

Jack's emotional withdrawal and coldness enveloped her. Had she said too much? As she took a breath and prepared to excuse herself, Blythe came to their rescue. She slid over and pressed against Kate, with her head on her friend's arm. "My mommy died. She was sick for a long time. She went to the hospital and never came home. I miss her a lot." Her tears dripped on Kate's arm.

"Oh, Blythe!" Kate put her arm around the little girl, wishing she could hug away Blythe's pain. "I'm sure you do. I'm so very sorry." Guilt engulfed Kate because, for a whole year, she had chosen not to see her mother. This little girl didn't have a choice. She pulled a clean napkin out of the dispenser and gently wiped away Blythe's tears.

Jack blinked and swallowed hard, as though willing himself not to break down as he watched her with his niece. He didn't comment and changed the subject.

He picked up his fork and asked, "Do you have family around here?"

She removed her arm from Blythe's shoulders. How much should she tell him? "No, my parents live several hours from here, in Mountain View. I work in the Mill Valley Florist shop."

He nodded. "I haven't been in the florist shop for a long time." Blythe snuggled against Kate as she smoothed hair back from the little girl's damp face. "Have we met before, I mean before this afternoon? Have you ever been in the computer store in Break-a-Bean?" She shook her head. He ate a couple of French fries. "Do you have brothers and sisters?"

"Yes, one brother. He has two children, a boy and a girl about your age, Blythe."

Blythe sat up and smiled. "Maybe I can play with them some time. What are their names?" She took a sip of lemonade and bit into a French fry.

"The boy is Cody, and the girl is Melissa. They don't live around here, but maybe you will get to meet them one day." She turned her attention back to the uncle. "How about you, Jack? Do you live in Millvale?"

He shook his head. "No, although I grew up here. I work at Clint's Computers over in Break-a-Bean, so I have an apartment there. It's close enough for me to help Mark with Blythe."

"Any other family?"

A shadow crossed Jack's face. He shook his head and avoided her eyes. "No, it's just Blythe and Mark and me. Our parents died several years ago in a plane crash. Blythe told you about her mother."

She reached across the table and touched his wrist. "I'm sorry."

He startled at her touch. Their eyes locked for a moment, as though their hearts connected through sorrow. The pain in his eyes made her wonder how much he suffered and if she should have asked about his family. Blythe's voice broke into the uncomfortable silence.

"Uncle Jack takes care of me when Daddy goes away." She chewed a bite of her hamburger and sipped lemonade. "Uncle Jack can help you with your computer if you have trouble."

She glanced at Jack and smiled. "I'll remember that, Blythe." The corners of his mouth turned up before he looked away.

"Do you like my house, Kate?"

Kate's thoughts took a moment to change directions, unlike Blythe's, which worked like a whirl-wind. "Oh, yes, I do." In her mind she pictured the cottage she had seen that afternoon. "Your house is charming." With a smile she added, "And you know what? I kept waiting for the Three Bears to walk out of it."

Blythe laughed with delight, and her uncle chuckled.

Jack gazed at her thoughtfully. "Haven't I seen you in Valley Community Church on Sundays?"

Kate shrugged. "Maybe. I go with Ellie Somers and her fiancé."

He snapped his fingers and smiled. "That's it! I've seen you with Ellie and Ben."

Kate attended church with Ellie out of habit, especially since Ellie prodded her to go. Within her self-imposed wall of isolation, Kate avoided involvement with church people or activities as much as possible. She hadn't noticed Jack or encouraged the attention of any young man.

On second thought, maybe she had seen Jack from a distance, and that was why he seemed familiar. Only a few people, like the insistent Mrs. Matthews, had broken through her wall. For the past year she had blamed God for Tim's death. Surely He could have stopped the drunk driver or spared Tim if He wanted to.

As she mulled this over in her mind, Kate noticed that her anger at God had ebbed away. She no longer had to blame Him. Her tears and talking about Tim had been a release.

She bent her head as she finished her dinner and thought about the future. She still had dreams, which now included getting to know this brown-eyed pixie and her handsome, blue-eyed uncle better.

LATER THAT EVENING, on the way back to the cottage, Jack and Blythe rode in silence, both lost in their own thoughts. The pain of Jack's own losses had surfaced when Kate cried. Did she live with bitterness too? He still felt unbalanced by the touch of her hand.

Blythe announced from the back seat, "Uncle Jack, I think you should marry Kate. I like her."

"Whoa!" Astonished, Jack peered at his niece in the rearview mirror then back at the road, still wet from the earlier rain. "Where did that thought come from? We just met her."

He hadn't paid attention to Ellie and Ben's quiet friend in church. Now he wanted to know everything about her. From the appearance of her painting, she had talent. And Blythe connected with her right away. Disappointed that his niece's doctor's appointment had prevented their further acquaintance earlier in the day, his heart beat faster when he saw her enter the diner.

Blythe's request to invite her to sit with them had not been a problem for him. When Kate agreed, he nearly skipped on the way back to join Blythe.

He pondered ways to accomplish seeing the pretty young

woman with blonde hair again without being obvious. In a small town, people would notice. In spite of his attraction to her, he didn't intend to ever marry or have a family. At least she wasn't engaged. He frowned. How selfish of him! She obviously didn't want another relationship if she still wore her dead fiancé's ring. But they could be friends.

Blythe persisted, "Didn't you like her?"

"Yes, I did. But I hardly know her." He tried to deny to himself that he felt more drawn to the artist than to any woman he'd ever known.

Blythe missed her mother. He wondered if that had brought on the marriage proposal. He grinned when he thought she might say the same thing to her father. Blythe could be quite outspoken and determined at times. He knew they both probably gave in to her too often, but this time Mark certainly wouldn't, in spite of her sweet entreating. Mark was still bound to his dead wife. Blythe probably could, however, charm a tiger into giving up his stripes.

He chuckled at the thought, hoping she didn't hear.

Blythe nodded and said knowingly, "I still think you should marry her."

Jack kept his eyes on the road and attempted to keep his mind on driving.

CHAPTER TWO

"So, what did you think?" Ellie asked at work the next morning.

"About what?" Kate critically examined the floral arrangement she worked on. She expected her friend would bring up the subject sooner or later.

Ellie looked up at Kate before placing a stem of baby's breath in her arrangement. "About the meadow, the place I sent you to paint."

"Nature's gallery, it's all you said and more." Kate rearranged the irises and added two ferns.

"Ben and I often take that road. It's a beautiful area. Did you paint anything?"

"That's what I went out there for," she responded calmly, reluctant to discuss her painting before completing it.

"Did you get inspired and create a masterpiece?"

Kate laughed. "You sound like my mother. It's not as quick as making a flower arrangement, but I made progress. I'll have to go back."

She gazed at her handiwork, turning the vase, giving a touch here and there. Although she enjoyed arranging flowers, she couldn't explain how painting refreshed and renewed her. Or express in words how it felt to see her brush strokes turn into a completed work. Besides, she didn't want to reveal other thoughts to her friend. Not yet.

The shop phone rang before Ellie could say more. Kate attached a card to her arrangement, placed it in the cooler, and started another as Ellie talked on the phone.

"Yes, Lexa. When is your wedding?" Ellie smiled as she listened. "Yes, Thursday at ten will be fine. 'Bye." She clicked off the phone.

"Yes!" She raised both fists in victory and then turned to her friend. "Lexa Smith wants us to do her wedding flowers! I have an appointment with Lexa and her mother on Thursday morning!" Ellie pushed a lock of dark hair out of her face and wrote the appointment in her green date book. She also entered it into her cell phone.

Kate's chest tightened slightly as she remembered the excitement of making her own wedding plans. "Oh, Ellie, the Smith wedding will be the event of the summer in Millvale!" She picked up some ferns. "Did you know about the Three Bears cottage out there?" Once she spoke the words, she wished she could take them back.

"Huh? What was that?" Ellie looked up from her phone.

"Yesterday I met a little girl and fell in love with her."

"Three Bears cottage? Oh, you must mean the Chambers' house. Blythe is sweet and friendly, but don't expect the same from Papa Bear. Mark is a good man, but he isn't over his wife's death yet."

Kate sighed and shook her head. "The poor man. No, I didn't meet him."

"I heard that Blythe's uncle Jack is taking care of her while her father is away on business." Her raised eyebrows and expectant look made Kate blush.

She placed the ferns in the vase. "I know. They told me."

"What's the matter, Katie?" Ellie teased with a smile. "Jack's a handsome fella, isn't he? He's single."

"Don't get any ideas. He was in a hurry to take Blythe to an appointment."

"Are you interested?"

"Ell-ie!" Kate repositioned some flowers and stepped back to look at the arrangement. "When I went to the diner last night, Blythe and Jack invited me to sit with them. It was fun." Yes, Jack piqued her interest but not as a topic for discussion with Ellie. She had to understand her own response to him before she could talk about him.

"It's time you had a little romance again. I know you loved Tim, but it's time to get on with your life, girl."

Kate bit back a sharp reply. She enjoyed working for her dear friend, the older sister of her college roommate, but some days it was hard to have a romantically minded boss.

"HARDLY ROMANTIC," she mumbled, referring to the encounter of the previous day. She placed the finished arrangement in the cooler. "I'm going to water the plants in the greenhouse." *****

While waiting for her clothes to dry at the Laundromat after work on Thursday, Kate read a notice on the bulletin board: "Millvale Community Center is looking for volunteers to help with children's programs." Kate wrote down the telephone number.

As she drove by the center on her way home, she noticed adults and children going in and out. The image of Blythe enjoying her painting flashed in her mind. On impulse, she stopped and went in.

The center was a large building. She passed a gymnasium where little girls practiced gymnastics. Happy shouts came from behind the door marked "pool." She found the office and filled out an extensive application. She scheduled an interview with the center's assistant director. Since the job involved children, she had to be fingerprinted for a background check.

Later she struggled with her loaded laundry basket through the door of her studio apartment and set the basket on the table. The unfinished meadow painting stood propped on one chair. The setting sun glowed through her living room window as she looked around the small space. She and Tim had planned to buy a house as soon as they could afford it. She wanted a room for her own studio, where it wouldn't matter if she spattered paint. The outdoors had to be her studio for now.

Kate curled into a corner of the sofa, watching the diamond in her ring sparkle in the sun's last rays. She twisted the ring, her connection to Tim and a barrier from attention of other young men. Had her encounter with Jack been a sign? Maybe Ellie was right, it was time for a change, to get on with her life. She still had dreams. Maybe she could have another chance to love and be loved. Guilt stabbed her. Would that be disloyal to Tim and his memory?

JACK'S HEART raced as he walked into the church auditorium on Sunday morning. He looked around, hoping she was there.

"Over here, Uncle Jack," Blythe called to him from their usual place in the fourth pew on the left side. He smiled at his niece, hiding his disappointment. He couldn't say, "No, wait a minute, I'm looking for Kate." He didn't want to be that obvious. He greeted other worshipers as he made his way to Blythe and Mark. Mark moved over so Jack could sit. Blythe pushed her way past her dad's legs to give Jack a hug. She wiggled her body between them on the pew.

"I'll need you to take care of Blythe a couple of days this week. I have a conference out of town on Wednesday and Thursday," Mark said.

This would be another opportunity to see Kate. "Works for me." Jack tried to pay attention as Blythe chatted to him while discreetly looking for Kate.

Blythe stood up and pointed. "She's over there, Uncle Jack."

She spoke loud enough for several people around them to smile and try to see who the girl pointed to. Jack's face became hot. He managed to follow Blythe's pointing finger to Kate, who sat next to Ellie and Ben on the other side of the room. Their eyes met, and Kate smiled. His heart did a flip-flop, the corners of his mouth turned up. He shifted his gaze to the front when he noticed nosey Mrs. Matthews watching him. If she caught on to his interest in Kate, everyone in Millvale would know.

Jack sang the hymns without comprehension. He vaguely remembered Blythe leaving to go to children's church. He opened his Bible and appeared to be listening to Pastor Clary's message. When the people around him stood for the final hymn, Mark leaned toward him. "Where have you been, Bro'?" He stood, his face burning. He hoped no one else noticed his distractedness or guessed the reason for it.

Jack looked around for Kate as Mark went to get his daughter from children's church. He found her standing next to Ellie and Ben in a group of young adults. By the time he made his way to her side of the church, Mrs. Matthews had snagged her. He could wait. He intended to invite Kate to join them for dinner after church, but he wanted to avoid nosey Mrs. Matthews.

By now Mark and Blythe should be ready to go. Jack continued out of the building to the parking lot, where his brother and niece were getting into their car. He followed them out of the parking lot in his car.

~

KATE ARRIVED at the center early on Tuesday afternoon, nearly two weeks after submitting her application. She had plenty of time to check supplies and make sure everything was ready for her eight budding art students. She didn't notice someone standing in the doorway until a voice called out, "Kate, you're here!"

She looked up from counting paintbrushes. "Blythe!" Kate knelt to greet the child. "Are you in this class? Oops!" She balanced herself with her hand on the floor before Blythe's hug could knock her over. She had seen Blythe or Jack only at a distance in church on Sunday. Jack had smiled at her, but she hoped he would have tried to say hello.

Blythe nodded. "Uh-huh. Daddy said I could. Are you the teacher?"

Kate stood up. "Yes." Blythe grabbed her hand and dragged over to meet an older version of Jack.

"Daddy, Daddy! This is Kate!"

"You must be the famous 'Kate the Painter' Blythe has been talking about. I'm Mark Chambers." He shook her hand, his smile not quite reaching his tired eyes.

Kate barely had time to respond when Blythe shouted, "Look everybody, this is my friend Kate! She's our teacher!" A breathless Kate greeted seven more small but enthusiastic students. She caught Mark's eye. Was he laughing at her? He waved as he left the room and greeted a middle-aged woman as she entered.

The woman, dressed with casual elegance in white capris and a powder blue knit top, clapped her hands. "Okay, children, give Miss Kate some breathing space!" As the children scrambled to sit at the table, she turned to Kate. "You're the young woman who works with Ellie Somers, aren't you? I've heard some good things about you. Thank you so much for volunteering to teach the children. I'm Celia Smith."

The woman must be Lexa's mother. She clasped the woman's offered hand. "This is a new experience for me, Mrs. Smith, but I'm looking forward to it."

The center's director gave her a comforting smile. "Oh, please call me Celia. We're both adults."

Celia helped Kate organize the class, gave her a student list on a clipboard, and left with the promise to check up on the class later.

~

THE NEXT MORNING Kate breezed into work. "Good morning," she lilted.

Ellie looked up. "Are you in love?"

Kate laughed. "Well, maybe with eight adorable future artists."

Ellie snapped her fingers. "Oh, that's right, you had your first painting class at the center. I take it that all went well."

"Super! Blythe Chambers is in the class. I met her father."

Ellie leaned across the counter toward Kate. "What did you think?"

"About Mark Chambers? He's okay, I guess." Kate shrugged and added, "We didn't get much time to talk. Talk about family resemblance. He and Jack look so much alike. Either one could pass for Blythe's father."

She checked the orders on the counter. "Which do you want done first, the arrangements or the greenhouse?"

Ellie threw up her hands. "There you go, changing the subject again. Take care of the transplants first, please." Kate headed for the greenhouse. "Oh, by the way, Ben and I have set our wedding date," Ellie added, twirling with excitement.

Kate responded to the news with a smile, although a twinge of sadness pinched her heart. She couldn't deny the envy. "I'm glad. When?"

"August 15. That way we can be back from our honeymoon before the fall rush."

Kate nodded, and Ellie continued, "Do you think you could handle things here for a week while I'm away? I'll be hiring part-time summer help, so you won't be alone. But I could close down."

"If you want me to work, that will be fine. I'd rather stay busy," Kate assured her.

"I thought you might like to go home to see your family," Ellie suggested.

Kate took a moment to consider Ellie's words. On one hand, she missed her parents. She wanted to see them and the rest of her family. Keeping in touch by phone wasn't the same as being there. However, she feared being drawn back into her old life and old memories, stuck reliving the past. Her life here lay open before her with new possibilities. She wasn't ready to return to Mountain View.

Kate shook her head firmly. "No. Thanks anyway. Millvale is my home now."

Ellie shrugged. "Well, let me know if you change your mind. Will you be my bridesmaid?"

"Really, Ellie, you want me?" She pointed to herself. "What about Alana? Isn't she coming?"

"My sister is some place in Africa right now. She's planning to come, but sometimes travel in Third World countries is unpredictable. We thought you could easily step into the position of honor if she didn't make it."

Kate reached over and hugged her friend. "Okay. Thank you for asking me, Ellie."

"We plan to get married in Millvale, at Valley Community Church and have Pastor Clary perform the ceremony. So, will you help me with wedding plans? Mom will be here next weekend, and we'll go shopping for a gown, but she can't come again until the wedding. She has to take care of Grandma, so it's hard for her to get away." Ellie's family had lived in Millvale until just a few years ago. "A lot of things Ben and I can do together, but some things Ben won't or can't do."

Kate nodded again. "Sure, I can help you." After all, she had planned a wedding before.

The bell over the door announced a customer.

"Oh, by the way, remember that Mothers' Day is this weekend. Expect to be really busy between now and the middle of June, especially Mothers' Day and Memorial Day." Ellie checked her calendar. "We have to do flowers for three other weddings this summer, but none as big as Lexa Smith's. And, of course, we can't forget graduations."

BY THE END OF MAY, Kate decided she had sold plants or flowers to everyone in Millvale. Memorial Day promised to be sunny and warm. Kate made a salad and packed her cooler. After slathering on plenty of sunscreen, she grabbed her sunglasses and straw hat. Crowds of people lined the curbs, waving small American flags, waiting for the parade to begin. Kate stopped to speak to Mr. and Mrs. Matthews and Pastor Clary and his family.

"Kate! Kate!" She spotted Blythe across the street, jumping up and down, waving both hands, one holding a flag. She smiled and waved back. Mark and Jack each raised a hand in greeting.

She quickly crossed the street. "Hi." She crouched down to give the little girl a hug.

"Do you like parades, Kate? I do, especially when they throw out lots of candy."

Quickly Mark said, "Blythe, they don't give candy for Memorial Day. This is a special day when we remember soldiers who have died for our country."

The girl twisted her mouth and placed a hand on her hip. "I know. But I still like the candy."

Jack chuckled. "Didn't you have to work today, Kate?" He focused a warm, blue gaze on her.

She liked hearing him say her name. She liked his smile and his blue eyes. Heat rushed to her cheeks when she realized she didn't answer his question. "No. I usually take Tuesday afternoons off for painting. Ellie gave me the whole day so I could come to the parade. She has a couple of college students helping her today."

"What are your plans for this afternoon?" he asked. "We're having a picnic."

Blythe jumped into their conversation. "Daddy, can Kate come to our picnic?"

Mark shrugged. "I guess you can ask her. She may have other plans."

"Will you join us, Kate?" Jack asked, and Blythe nodded eagerly.

With a twinge of regret, she said, "Oh, thank you for your invitation, but I already have plans. I'm meeting Ellie and Ken for a picnic. I'm sorry." She indicated the cooler beside her.

"Oh." Blythe's shoulders drooped.

Mark touched his daughter's cheek. "Maybe Kate will join us another time, honey." They heard the steady beat of drums, the bright blare of trumpets, and the blend of musical sounds as the band played in the distance. Blythe pointed as she caught sight of the approaching military color guard, marching in time, flags fluttering. She took Kate's hand, and warmth spread over Kate as she stood with the Chambers family to watch the parade pass by. She breathed in the spicy scent of Jack's after shave as he stood on her other side. Several times she looked up and caught him watching her. They both quickly turned their eyes back to the parade. She heard the murmur of Mark's voice as he quietly explained the commemoration to Blythe.

They followed the parade to the town's war memorial statue. After the VFW commander read the list of veterans from the community who had died and a trumpeter played "Taps," they said their goodbyes.

"Well, Pumpkin, I guess it's picnic time," Mark said to his daughter. "It was good to see you, Kate. Have a good afternoon."

Blythe reached for her father's hand. "I wish you could eat with us, Kate."

Kate's warm smile included the trio. "Maybe another time."

"Next time we'll have to plan ahead," Jack suggested. "Kate's a busy lady. We should have asked sooner. She will be joining us at the diner on Sunday, right, Kate?"

"That's right. And we'll have fun feeding the ducks like we did last week."

Blythe's face brightened.

"Remember, Blythe, I have to get ready to leave this evening." Mark touched his daughter's cheek.

Kate picked up her cooler. If Mark had to leave, maybe she could see more of Jack.

"Again?" Blythe grumbled.

"It's only for a couple of days this time. I'll be home Friday. We'll do something special this weekend, okay?"

The little girl twisted her mouth. "Okay."

Thoughts of Jack's blue eyes and heart-stopping smile kept popping up in her mind as she met Ellie and Ben and two other couples from church in the park for a picnic. She determined not to moon over Jack, and she refused to bemoan her own single state as she played with the young children of one of the couples. It was time to start making good memories again.

"THE JEWEL NECKLINE and cap sleeves are perfect for you, Ellie. And the color is right for your complexion." Kate slid into the passenger seat of Ellie's car after Ellie's second dress fitting. The cream-colored satin gown looked beautiful on her friend.

"Thanks, Kate. I really liked it, and my mother did too. What about the gowns I showed you for you and Alana? Did you like the color and style?" Ellie checked her mirrors and the traffic, put on her blinker, and pulled out into the street.

"I think they're a good choice. The jade is lovely. I think Alana will approve."

"It's a little hard getting her ideas since she's somewhere in Africa. Maybe I can send a picture to her on the cell phone. I want her to feel included."

"That's a good idea."

Ellie stopped at a four-way stop and waited for her turn to proceed. "How about some ice cream? I'll treat."

Kate licked her lips. "Make that Dutch treat, and you have a deal. We'd better go easy on the ice cream this summer. Valerie won't like making changes to your gown at the last minute." They giggled.

Seated at a small, umbrella-shaded table outside the ice cream shop, they licked their cones. The light traffic on the street left moments when they heard the barking of a dog in someone's yard and the shrieks of children at play. They greeted a family who entered the ice cream shop and waved to a few passers-by. Kate sat back, enjoying the sweet flavor of her raspberry swirl cone and the coolness of the ice cream as it slid down her throat.

"Hi, Miss Kate!" A girl and her mother paused by their table.

Kate sat up. "Why, hello, Serena. How are you today?"

"I'm fine. I can't wait to show Mommy my paintings."

"You've worked hard. I'm sure your mother will love them." The mother's smile assured Kate this would be so.

"Serena has enjoyed your class. She's already asking if she can join it again next summer."

"I hope so. I have enjoyed teaching Serena and the others."

"We're going shopping." Serena hopped on one foot and then

the other. "When we're finished, we're coming back for ice cream."

"Have fun!" They left, and Kate sat back.

"Mmm. This is so good!" Ellie closed her eyes as she tasted her ice cream. "How is your painting class?"

"My young artists are talented, especially Blythe. She shows real potential. I have to be careful not to favor her. They're all getting paintings ready for the open house on July 4."

"You enjoy teaching them."

"I love them. They are so much fun! They listen to my instructions and work hard. Volunteering for the class is one of the best decisions I've made."

Kate finished her cone and leaned her elbows on the table. "And I've learned a lot working with you. Making flower arrangements has improved my painting. I'm more aware of subtle differences in colors and shapes. And it has been fun planning and making wedding arrangements with you."

"Lexa loves our ideas for her flowers. I've really appreciated your help." Ellie finished the last bite of her cone and wiped her fingers on a napkin. "Does it bother you to do the flowers for others' weddings?"

Kate searched her mind and heart before answering. "To be honest, I won't say I don't have bits of envy from time to time." She rubbed her fingertips across the table top. "It hasn't always been easy hearing other women discuss wedding plans. It doesn't hurt as much now. A year ago, when I came here, I was locked in the past. I thought I'd never be happy again. Now I can look forward and make plans for the future." She rested her hand over Ellie's hand on the table. "I'm so happy for you and Ben. I know you'll have a wonderful marriage. I'm fine, really. I've had so much fun being your wedding planner."

"You've been spending time with Jack lately."

She pushed her hair behind her ears. "Yes, Blythe always seems to have something she wants us to do with her. Jack says she insists on inviting me. Blythe makes life an adventure. Did you hear her comments about your house the other day when I brought her to see it?" Kate had enjoyed viewing Ellie and Ben's new home though Blythe's eyes.

"Ben and I nearly doubled over with laughter when she suggested where we could put our children and how many could fit into the house. She had some pretty funny ideas about colors and decorating as well." Ellie placed her hand against her cheek and laughed.

"Yes, she's not afraid to speak her mind. But she's so sweet and funny and sincere when she does it, you don't mind. I feel God has used Blythe to help me enjoy living again."

"What about Jack?"

Kate brushed a speck from her t-shirt. "You're wondering where Jack and I are going?" Kate wadded her napkin as Ellie nodded. "I don't know if there's a future for Jack and me. It's like he's drawn a line, and I can't step across it to get any closer, not that I want to rush into a more serious relationship. I just don't know."

"In all the years I've known Jack, I don't remember him seriously dating anyone, although a lot of girls tried to get his attention. Do you think he's afraid of commitment?"

Kate shrugged. "Maybe. I'm not sure why. But since I'm not ready yet anyway, it's okay. I like Jack. He's fun and considerate, and he loves that little girl as though she were his own."

"His father was a good man. Both boys resemble their father, including their looks."

Kate smiled. "Yes, Jack's an attractive man. I haven't known him long, so there's no hurry." A longing for something more tugged at her heart. She leaned forward and rested her arms on the table. "Now, what's the next thing on your 'to-do for the wedding' list?"

Jack's actions puzzled her. On one hand, he appeared to enjoy spending time with her. On the other hand, he held her at arm's length. The pieces of the puzzle did not fit together, at times, confusing and frustrating her. Kate didn't want to talk about Jack right now, but that didn't mean his blue eyes and heart-stopping smile didn't invade her thoughts or peace of mind.

CHAPTER THREE

ate followed Blythe to a patch of wild strawberries on the edge of the meadow. She should be painting and preparing for her class this afternoon, not picking strawberries with Blythe. She found it hard to say no to the little girl.

Berry baskets in hand, they picked for only a minute when the little girl lifted Kate's left hand. "What happened to your ring?"

"Huh?" The unexpected question made Kate pause for a moment to look at the ring's impression still visible on her finger. Blythe's wrinkled brow indicated her concern. "I took it off and put it in a safe place. I don't need it to help me remember Tim anymore." Although she had decided it was time to put it away so she could move forward with her life, her finger still felt strange and empty without it.

Blythe shrugged. "I thought maybe you lost it. It's so pretty." She turned her attention back to wild strawberries. "Mommy and I used to pick wild strawberries. She showed me how." She took a deep breath and continued. "Did you know my mommy's name was Rachael, like in the Bible? She was so pretty. Sometimes I almost forget what she looked like. Then I look at her picture and miss her a lot." She bit her lip and became very still.

Kate laid her hand on Blythe's shoulder. "I feel that way too. Tim was very special to me. I think it's okay to be sad sometimes when we remember. But when we remember the good things about a person and the good times we had, it helps."

"I remember lots of good things. My mommy was nice. Now she's in heaven with Jesus. Sometimes I think about how happy she is there." She looked across the meadow with a far-away gaze. "I still miss her."

Kate drew the little girl into a hug. She chuckled, though, when she noticed Blythe's berry-stained face. "Make sure you save some berries for your daddy."

"I will," Blythe assured her. She picked a few more berries. "Sometimes at night I hear Daddy crying. I think he still misses Mommy. I want to go in and hug him and help him feel better, but he doesn't like for me to get out of bed. I used to have bad dreams, but I sleep better now." She moved to a spot with more berries. "Uncle Jack won't talk about Mommy either."

The child's sensitivity and perceptiveness amazed her. "Blythe, thank you for telling me about your mother. She was a special person, and you loved her very much." Blythe nodded, and Kate added, "I'm glad you invited me to come berry-picking with you."

The little girl responded with a pink, berry-stained grin. "Me too."

As she had promised, Blythe helped Kate prepare for the class at the community center and afterwards helped Kate clean up as well. She had just placed the last jar of paint on the shelf and closed the cupboard door when a man's voice said, "Can I help?"

"Uncle Jack! Look, Kate, it's Uncle Jack!" Blythe ran and threw her arms around his neck as he bent to greet her.

He whirled her around and said, "It looks like you enjoyed your wild strawberries." He took a paper towel, wetted it, and tried to rub the stain from the girl's face.

"I already washed my face. Want some strawberries? Kate and I shared." She ran to get a small, plastic dish from the table.

"I'm surprised you had any left." He took two and popped them into his mouth. "You'd better save the rest for your daddy. He likes them too."

Blythe grinned and replaced the lid.

"This is a surprise. I didn't know you were coming." Butterflies danced in Kate's stomach. She brushed at some lint on her paint smock.

"There's a men's Bible study tonight. I thought I'd come early and see if you wanted to go to the diner for dinner."

Although the unexpected invitation sent a thrill through her, Kate tried to react calmly. She reached up to straighten the moist paintings that hung from paper clips attached to a wire. "Well, yes, that sounds nice. I didn't have any special plans."

"Me, too, Uncle Jack?"

"Of course, Princess. Your daddy had some extra work at the office this afternoon, so he said you may come with us."

"Oh, goody! We can watch the ducks!"

Wishing for time alone with Jack, Kate swallowed her disappointment, smiled, and said, "I'll be ready in a minute. Blythe has been a great help today, so everything's done." Kate took off her smock and hung it on a hook on the cupboard door. "There." She looked around the room, "All set." She lifted her quilted bag.

"After you, mesdemoiselles." Jack bowed with a sweep of his hand toward the door.

Blythe giggled, and Kate smiled as Jack closed the door behind them.

Outside, after their meal, Jack pulled a plastic bag of dried bread crusts from his jacket pocket. "Here, Ducky," he said to his niece, "feed the ducks."

"Okay, Uncle Jack. Thanks."

"Be careful. We don't want to fish you out of the pond."

"I'll be careful," she promised.

Kate sat on the park bench beside Jack as they watched Blythe. Her earlier conversation with Blythe about her mother weighed heavily on her mind. "Jack, Blythe talked to me about her mother. How long has Rachael been gone?"

Jack didn't answer right away, and Kate wondered if he would. He stared at his hands as his jaw worked. "Rachael died about two years ago."

"I see," she said softly. "She must have been a wonderful person. Blythe has many good memories."

His eyes met hers, his eyebrows raised. "I'm surprised she talked to you about her mother. She doesn't talk much about her."

"She did that night at the diner, remember? Do you ever talk to her about Rachael?" When Jack shook his head, she said, "Blythe is sensitive. I think she thinks you'll get mad if she talks about her."

"I never considered . . . It's hard to talk about her." Jack picked up a small stone and tossed it into the water.

For a couple of minutes they sat in silence, watching Blythe talking to the ducks. So much of what they said and did revolved around Blythe. Kate wanted to talk about them, to know how Jack really felt about her. She wished she could read his mind. Did he ever think about them? About getting married and having a family?

JACK CHECKED HIS WATCH. He knew about Kate's family, but she didn't talk much about her past. Neither did he. Often Blythe carried their conversations. It was easier not to become too personal that way. Now he wanted to know more about her. He needed to sort through his feelings for the woman beside him, who painted so skillfully, loved his niece, and interested him as no other woman had.

"Tell me about Tim." Sometimes he felt that Tim was his competition for her affection. That was ridiculous, however, because Tim was dead, and he didn't plan to marry Kate. When she hesitated, he wanted to take the words back.

She looked at him and started to speak, but she looked away. He opened his mouth to apologize and change the subject when she turned back at him.

She tucked a lock of hair behind her ear. "What do you want to know?"

He leaned forward on his elbows. "How did you two meet?"

"We grew up together, sort of. We went to the same church. He and my brother were friends, and they played sports together. Kevin was a little older than Tim." The corners of her mouth turned up. "Actually, I didn't really like him very much. I thought he was a show-off, and he liked to tease me."

Jack grinned. He did his share of teasing in high school. "So, what changed your mind?"

"I discovered we shared an interest in art. He liked making pottery. I liked to paint."

"He had a pottery business?"

"No, he sold insurance. He liked people, and he was a good salesman. He discovered he liked making pottery and learned to use a potter's wheel. He did that for enjoyment and relaxation." She reached for the ring no longer on her finger. "He said it reminded him that God was in charge of his life, like the potter who forms the clay into useful pottery. His favorite verse was Isaiah 64:8. 'But now, O Lord, You are our Father; We are the clay, and You our potter; And all we are the work of Your hand.'" She brushed a wrinkle from her capris.

"How long were you engaged?" He watched the breeze playing with strands of Kate's honey-colored hair, longing to touch them.

She brushed her hair off her cheek. "Six months. But we knew each other a lot longer than that." She smiled. "Tim loved to tease and have fun. He made me laugh. Beneath what I thought was shallowness was a thoughtful, caring person. His younger sister adored him." She gazed at the ducks on the pond. "Sometimes it hurts to remember Tim, but I have good memories. Just like Blythe has good memories of her mother." Blythe waved to her, and she waved back. "I'll never forget him and what we had, but I'm ready to go on with my life."

Her eyes met his, and he looked away first. "Do you ever wonder why God makes masterpieces and then allows them to die? It's as though the potter smashes his own creations."

They both started when the mother duck quacked, and Blythe giggled.

Kate took a deep breath. "Tim's death made me think a lot about life and death. I don't understand why Tim had to die, and I blamed God for a long time. I kept thinking that God could have stopped it. I felt as though Tim's life had been wasted."

"I felt that way after my parents died." His confession to Kate surprised him. Only Mark knew how much he had struggled with that tragedy, with anger and hopelessness and questions. The same feelings resurfaced when Rachael died. "How do you feel now?"

Kate spoke slowly, as though choosing the right words to express her thoughts. "I still don't understand why it happened. I left Mountain View because everything reminded me of Tim. I've had a lot of time to think and put what happened in perspective. You know, Jack, Tim isn't broken pottery. He's whole in heaven with Jesus. I think those of us left behind, Tim's family, me, are the broken ones, who are being made over into something more useful to God."

Jack steepled his fingers and leaned forward to rest his chin on them. "Rachael was one of God's masterpieces. She was perfect for Mark and as a mother for Blythe." He shook his head. "I don't understand why God took away that little girl's mother. She didn't deserve this."

"I know," Kate said softly. "Blythe loved her mother very much, and from what she has told me, they were very close. I think Rachael would be proud of Blythe. She's a special little girl."

Jack nodded and swallowed hard.

Kate continued. "I didn't want to accept comfort from other people at first. I just wanted to be angry, at Tim, at God, it didn't matter. Leaving Mountain View may have been the right choice for the wrong reason. I wanted to run away from the pain, but it didn't work. I've had a lot of time to work through the pain. Sometimes I'm sad when I think about Tim, but the anger is gone." She added, "Maybe one day I can help someone else suffering from the loss of a loved one."

Jack's gaze met hers. He smiled. "You've helped Blythe."

Tears filled her eyes as she held out her hand toward Blythe. "Blythe has helped me too. Maybe it's because we've both been broken pottery."

He took her hand and squeezed it, which sent a shock up his arm. He pulled his hand back. "It's time to go. The Bible study begins in a few minutes." He needed time to process Kate's words. She obviously had a different perspective on death than he had. Like him, she had struggled, but her faith shone like the sparkle of the diamond in her ring, the ring that no longer encircled the ring finger on her left hand. When had she removed it, and why?

She stood. "Okay. Thank you for dinner."

❧

HAD her words helped Jack at all? Kate could only hope.

He surprised her when he called her later. "There's a church softball game on Saturday afternoon. I wondered if you would go with me. Mark's bringing Blythe with him."

Kate put down her book. "Well, I'm not very good, and I haven't played for quite a while, but I think I remember how. What time?"

"I'll pick you up at one-thirty. The game starts at two."

"Okay. Sounds like fun. Should I bring something to eat?"

"Sure. There's going to be a church picnic, and there will be other activities as well. Everyone is supposed to bring something to eat."

After she hung up from the call, Kate tried to read again. She had decided to splurge on the book to reward herself and inspire her painting. The expensive book, on artists and their painting techniques, also included some examples of beautiful paintings. Unable to concentrate any longer, she closed the book.

What did Jack's invitation mean? Would they become more than friends? She hoped so. They had spent quite a lot of time together, but this was the first time it felt like a date, like Jack wanted to show they were a couple. She pulled her knees up to her chin and wrapped her arms around them.

BLYTHE AND MARK arrived at the field before them on Saturday afternoon. Blythe ran up to her friend and threw her arms around her waist. "Uncle Jack said you were coming too. Daddy's here, and I'm going to play over there with my friends. Bye." She gave Jack a quick hug and flitted away to join a group of children playing on the playground.

Kate looked at Jack, and they burst out laughing. "That's my niece!" he said.

Without responsibility for Blythe, they had more time for

each other and for talking with other couples. Kate knew Dave and Donna Campbell from the Memorial Day picnic, where she had played with their children. Matt and Kelly Sampson, a new couple who had just moved to Millvale, were expecting their first child at the end of the summer. Nate and Laura Betts had organized the activities. They had a gift for making everyone feel welcome. She enjoyed getting to know the people at the first church social event she attended since coming to Millvale. Their church friends, including Ellie and Ben, apparently considered them a couple. She didn't mind for herself, but what about Jack?

Mrs. Matthews, the church's self-appointed news gatherer and sometimes gossip, stopped Jack. Whatever she said, Jack nodded and blushed. He kept stepping back until he could break away from the talkative woman. He shook his head as he approached Kate. Her smile faded and a teasing comment died from her lips when she saw the angry set of his mouth.

"The old biddy is so nosey. 'I see you brought Kate Greenway today. That is so nice. It's about time you. . .'" Jack stopped abruptly.

Kate couldn't resist asking, "You what?" She thought she knew why Jack left the sentence unfinished, but she wanted Jack to say it.

"Never mind." He took her hand. "I'm sorry, Kate. I don't mean to be disrespectful, but I wish she would mind her own business."

Disappointed by Jack's response, Kate nodded. Sometimes Mrs. Matthews did ask too many questions, but Kate thought she meant well. "Mr. Matthews calls his wife an incurable romantic and matchmaker. He's tried to break her of matchmaking, but she figures their fifty years of marriage make her an expert." She stopped and bit her lip. Had she said too much? She couldn't tell by Jack's expression. She didn't want her time with Jack spoiled by worrying about what others said about them. She patted his arm. "We won't let Mrs. Matthews ruin our fun."

Jack gave Kate a crooked smile, shrugged, and nodded.

Kate had plenty of help remembering the things she had forgotten about softball. As Jack and the other guys on the team willingly advised her how to play, she ground her teeth and refrained from throwing down her bat as their advice bordered on bossiness.

"Step closer to the plate, Kate."

"Hold the bat higher, Kate."

"Watch the ball, Kate."

Breathing deeply, determined to do it right, she struck out twice before making two base hits. In the fifth inning she managed to reach home plate for a run. As she cheered and high-fived team mates, Jack's arms surrounded her waist, and he twirled her around.

Kate enjoyed watching the good-natured rivalry between the Chambers brothers, who belonged to opposing teams. From a distance they could pass for twins. Of similar build, just under six feet tall, with strong, fit bodies, they both loved to play softball. As she watched, Kate experienced the sensation of tumbling head-over-heels for the younger brother.

Kate and Jack's team squeezed out a win by one run. The day ended with a picnic supper accompanied by a lot of playful antics, noisy banter, and laughter. Ben led a short devotional from the Psalms. The orange sun lay on the western horizon when the church fellowship broke up that evening.

Blythe ran up to Kate. "Daddy said I could ask you to come to a picnic at our house on July 4. At night we can go to the fireworks too. Will you come, Kate? Please? Uncle Jack wants you to come too."

Kate looked at Jack. His smile invited her. Mark confirmed the invitation.

"I'd love to, Blythe. Thank you for asking me."

The little girl clapped her hands. "Uncle Jack said I had to ask early because you're a busy lady."

"I did say that, didn't I?" he said with a grin.

Kate lay awake for a long while that night, thinking about Jack, trying to piece together their relationship, asking for God's guidance. If she could only read Jack's mind. Sleep finally claimed her, her dreams filled with Jack.

CHAPTER FOUR

*I*n preparation for Lexa Smith's late June wedding, Kate and Ellie talked and dreamed flower arrangements in coral, ice yellow, and white. Kate gave up her afternoon to paint during the week before the wedding. For two days they worked long hours creating all the corsages, boutonnieres, bouquets, and arrangements of cascading variegated ivy, lilies, carnations, roses, and baby's breath. Ellie hired a part-timer to help with the regular business.

Their hard work paid for itself. The talents of the two young women, Kate's artistic skill and Ellie's knowledge of flowers, complemented each other.

Celia Smith called the shop on Monday morning after the wedding. "The arrangements were absolutely stunning! You girls did a marvelous job! Lexa was thrilled, and many of our guests commented. You can be sure I'll recommend Mill Valley Florist to my acquaintances."

"Thank you, Celia." Ellie smiled at Kate. Kate signaled a thumbs-up.

Business at the shop increased as the reputation of Mill Valley Florist grew. Ellie kept her part-time worker as a regular employee. It appeared they would have a busy fall as well, with flowers ordered for several weddings, anniversaries, and other celebrations. Kate's life became busy and full.

More and more Blythe's uncle filled her thoughts and her heart. Their softball "date" had not brought more romance into their relationship, to her disappointment. Whether they had dinner out or went to a movie, they went swimming or had a picnic, Blythe or someone else went with them. Although they had fun together, and she thought Jack liked being with her, he never hinted at a future for them. Whenever someone mentioned a wedding or a new baby, he became quiet.

Even though she loved Blythe and enjoyed spending time with her, she wanted to go out to dinner with Jack without an audience. She longed for his arms around her and wondered how it would feel to be kissed by him. She wanted to know that he loved her and wanted to be more than friends.

Maybe God was telling her it was too soon for her to fall in love again.

HE TRIED to deny his growing love for her. His resistance weakened. Kate didn't force herself on him, like other women tried to do. He liked being with her. He didn't need his niece to remind him how sweet, pretty, and talented she was. At times he pictured Kate as a permanent addition to his life. The image scared him. What if he declared himself, and then she walked away or died? Could he trust her with his heart? Did he really want the entanglement? He couldn't walk away.

Blythe adored her. As he spent more time with Kate, he used Blythe's presence to block greater intimacy. Kate didn't seem to mind, although at times he caught a facial expression he couldn't decipher that made him wonder what she was thinking and wanted to say.

Jack liked working for his boss, but he dreamed of owning a computer store in Millvale. He spent hours on the computer at night, finding information about on-line courses and small business loans. His research allowed brief respites from thinking about Kate.

All week his heart beat faster each time the door opened at Clint's Computers, only to have his hopes dashed when her face didn't appear. He tried to think of an excuse to stop in at Mill Valley Florist, disappointed that Ellie didn't have a computer problem for him to fix.

Late one afternoon, he stopped to see his brother at his office. He briefly shared some information about his business research then opened the subject he wanted to discuss.

"Mark, I'd like to set up a picnic table at the meadow. Is that all right with you?"

"Are we having a picnic?" Mark's face held an amused and thoughtful expression.

"Well, Blythe and Kate both like the meadow. And Kate likes to draw and paint there. I thought a table might be a good place for her supplies. We could hang up a swing for Blythe too."

"Hmm. This sounds serious." He tapped a pen on his desk.

Jack waited for Mark to comment about his relationship with Kate, relieved when he didn't. He trusted that his brother wouldn't make his interest in Kate public knowledge.

"I found a table on sale. Will you help me get it and put it up?"

"I think both your ideas are good ones, especially if you plan to spend more time there. Do you want to do it now?"

"If you have time. I'd like to have it set up by Saturday afternoon."

"I'll be finished here in about five minutes. I have to pick Blythe up from day care, then we can go."

"Thanks, Bro'." With excitement he anticipated Kate's reaction, even though it wasn't the indoor studio she longed for.

On Saturday afternoon, Kate met Jack and Blythe at the meadow. Blythe ran to hug Kate as she got out of her car. Blythe talked non-stop, gesturing with her hands. She pointed to the picnic table and swing. As Jack waited for them, he couldn't see Kate's expression clearly, but her voice expressed pleasure and surprise. Blythe lifted Kate's quilted bag to her shoulder and staggered, but she refused to give it back to Kate. Jack chuckled. Kate usually carried her sketchbook and drawing supplies in her bag. The only time he had seen her without it was at church on Sunday.

His breath caught as they approached him. Her face glowed, and the knit top she wore, although modest, accentuated her slender figure. Her hair fell softly around her face. Her eyes connected with his, and he felt lost in their green depths. He couldn't deny he loved her.

Unsure how long they stood there letting their eyes speak, a hand grasped his arm and shook it. "Uncle Jack, will you push me on my swing?"

Reluctantly he pulled his eyes away from Kate's. His body trembled, and it took a moment to return to reality and Blythe.

"Sure, princess." He glanced at Kate, who stood beside the table and ran her fingertips over the surface. Blythe pulled him over to the swing and hopped on. He gave her a huge push, and she squealed with glee. Kate sat. Her eyes followed his movements.

She took out her sketch book and pencils and began to draw. Jack left Blythe and sat next to Kate. He loved that she allowed him to watch her draw and paint. Like magic, details of faces and objects appeared. Him pushing Blythe on the swing. The meadow with its summer blooms. The spruce trees. The sky and clouds. He reveled in her closeness, although careful not to bump her arm.

"Your turn, Kate." Blythe hopped off the swing. Between the two of them, they convinced her to try it.

He challenged them to a bubble-blowing contest, handing out a bottle of bubble soap to each of them. "The one who blows the biggest bubble gets to choose the first candy bar." He held out three.

He couldn't keep his eyes off her. He didn't want the afternoon to end.

He didn't tell her about his inner war between love and fear.

On the Fourth of July, Kate joined the Chambers family as they attended the open house at the Community Center. They viewed Blythe's paintings on display and talked with Kate's other students and their parents.

Kate was proud of all her students and felt like a member of the community now, counting among her friends the parents of the children she taught, members of the church, and customers at the shop. The clouds from her storm caused by Tim's death had raced away in the warmth and brightness of her new life, and she thanked God.

After the morning parade in Millvale and their picnic at noon at Mark's cottage, they drove to Break-a-Bean to watch fireworks. The town, decked out in red, white, and blue, celebrated the Fourth with a carnival and craft fair. Kate and Jack perused the craft booths while Mark took his daughter on the rides. Kate found some gifts for her family, and Jack won a teddy bear for her when he hit every target at the shooting booth.

As darkness settled over the town, the little girl cuddled up with her father on one blanket to watch the fireworks show. Kate and Jack sat together on a second one. She appreciated this time "alone" with Jack. Kate observed the families around her and greeted several children and their parents from her painting class. Friends from church and customers from the flower shop also stopped to greet them. Jack introduced her to several of his coworkers and spoke to store customers. Kate gazed at Blythe and Mark, and sighed.

Jack leaned closer. "Is everything okay, Kate?" His breath tickled her neck.

When she turned her head, their noses almost touched. Her stomach flip-flopped. "I'm just thinking."

"About what?" His fingers gently brushed a wayward lock of hair from her cheek. His eyes traveled from her eyes to her lips and back.

Kate closed her eyes and leaned into his touch.She searched his face in the waning light. "Do you really want to know?" His blue gaze drew her in.

Jack nodded. "Of course."

Kate pulled up her knees and rested her chin on them before responding. "I hope one day I'll have a beautiful little girl like Blythe. Tim and I wanted a large family. I hope God will give me a second chance."

To Kate's surprise and confusion, Jack's arm came around her shoulders, and he pulled her against him. Their eyes locked. His smile made her heart beat faster. She trembled and took a shivery breath.

"All of us have dreams." His fingertips brushed her cheek.

Nearby someone shouted, "Look at that!"

He abruptly removed his arm from her shoulders and clasped his hands around his knees.

A sudden chill made Kate rub her arms. Why did Jack do that? The shouter wasn't referring to them, probably couldn't see them in the dim light. His fickle behavior left her confused, uncertain. Was Jack playing games with her feelings, or had he briefly revealed his true attraction for her? Was she expecting too much too soon in their relationship?

How long did she have to wait?

The pop of two Roman candles signaled the start of the fire-works show amid the "oh's" and "ah's" of the crowd of spectators. Cuddling her bear between her body and bent knees, Kate wrapped her arms around them, determined not to make herself vulnerable again. She had opened her heart to Jack, and he had shut the door to his. The warmth and glow of the evening had faded, but she determined she would enjoy the sparkling display before her.

❧

As Kate prepared for her class on Tuesday of the following week, Celia Smith entered the art room. "Mark Chambers called to say that his daughter is ill and won't be coming to class today,"

"Hmm. She seemed fine on Sunday. I'll miss her. Did he say what's wrong?" Kate handed Celia a short list of supplies she needed to restock.

Celia glanced at the paper. "He didn't say, but that little girl has inherited her mother's weakness for respiratory problems."

Kate knew little about Rachael Chambers and less about Mark and Jack's parents. Ellie had told her a few things. Reluctant to discuss romantic relationships with her employer, she avoided asking Ellie too many questions.

"Did you know the Chambers family well?" Kate asked Celia. She hoped to be able to understand Jack better without gossiping.

"We were acquainted, but not close, although the family lived in Millvale for years. It was a tragedy when the boys' parents were killed in a plane crash several years ago. The boys have done remarkably well since then, but Mark's wife died a couple of years ago." She shook her head. "So much loss for them." She examined Kate's list. "I'll order these things right away. You should have them next week."

"Thanks, Celia." Kate turned to greet her arriving students and their parents, but she couldn't get her mind off Blythe.

49

After class, she picked up her phone to call the Chambers'
home. No, Jack might be there. Still smarting from his rejection
of her on the Fourth, she hadn't seen or talked to him except at
church. Mark would let her know if Blythe's illness was serious.

She wouldn't worry. Her nephew and niece often caught
colds and other viruses. All young children did. Blythe had been
healthy, without even a sniffle, since she had known her. She
prayed for her Tuesday night and Wednesday morning.

Kate had little time to think about Blythe the next day, with
the frequent ringing of the telephone and the busy customer
traffic at the shop. If someone at the mid-week service that
evening didn't have an update about Blythe, Kate would have to
call or stop by the house to check up on her little friend, even if it
meant talking to Jack. Her resolve went untested because Jack
reported to the congregation that Blythe was improving.

She met Ellie at the door of the florist shop the next morning.
"Have you heard any more about Blythe?" They entered
together.

"Not since last night. Jack said she was getting better. I
haven't heard differently, so I guess she's okay."

"I thought maybe Jack called you. Is everything okay
between you two? You didn't have much to say to each other last
night."

Kate walked behind the counter to put her quilted bag away
in the back room. "We've both been busy."

"That's all?" Ellie listened well and gave good advice.
Perhaps she could help Kate untangle the threads of her relationship with Jack.

A car pulled into the parking lot. Regret and relief warred
within Kate. "I think we have a customer."

"Yes, well, if you want to talk, I'm here."

"I know."

～

GREAT CONCERN for Blythe did not enter her thoughts until she saw Jack's sober face when she opened the door at his knock on the following Sunday morning. She didn't expect to find him at her door. He stood with his shoulders hunched and his hands in his pockets.

"Jack, what's the matter?"

"Blythe's in the hospital."

Her eyes widened. "Oh no, I didn't know! Why didn't you call me? You seemed to think she had a bad cold and was getting better on Wednesday. How serious is it?"

"Bad enough. I've never seen her like this. She has pneumonia." He looked up at her, pleading in his eyes. "Will you go with me to the hospital to see her this afternoon, over in Wellsburg? She's been asking for you." He looked down and scuffed his toe on the carpet.

Kate's overflow of love and concern for the little girl replaced her resentment of the distance created between them at the Fourth of July fireworks. She nodded. "Of course, Jack. I'll go with you." She saw the pain in his eyes. How could she say no to his request, even though she knew he might hurt her again?

He let out his breath. "Why don't you ride with me to church this morning? We can leave for the hospital from there."

After a pause, she nodded. "I guess that will be all right." She almost added, "If you can stand to be with me that long." She picked up her purse and Bible and followed him out to his car.

Pastor Clary included Blythe in his prayer that morning. When the sermon began, Jack took Kate's hand, which he had never done in church before. Kate, distracted, found it hard to concentrate on the pastor's words. She squeezed Jack's hand, and the corners of his mouth turned up in a slight smile that didn't quite reach his pain-filled eyes. She prayed silently. She didn't want to mistake Jack's emotional vulnerability for something more personal.

On the way out, Jack stopped to speak with Pastor Clary. Feeling a pressure on her arm, Kate turned to find Mrs. Matthews beside her. Kate considered her a faithful friend and prayer warrior, not sharing Jack's opinion of the older woman as a nosey busybody. "Hello, Mrs. Matthews."

"Hello, my dear. Will you please tell the Chambers boys that I'm praying for that little girl? She is such a dear." Tears stood in Mrs. Matthews' eyes.

Kate patted the older woman's hand. "I'll be sure to tell them. I know they appreciate everyone's love and concern."

"I've known those boys since they were babies. They think I'm just a busybody. But there's more in here than they think." Mrs. Matthews laid her hand over her heart. "I pray for them all the time because I care about them." The woman sniffed and pulled a hanky out of her purse to wipe her eyes.

Kate put her arm around Mrs. Matthews's shoulders and squeezed. "They know you care, I'm sure. And Blythe needs all the prayer she can get."

Mrs. Matthews patted her hand. "You're good for that boy, Kate Greenway. I'm glad he has you to lean on right now, along with the Lord Jesus. I'm praying for both of you."

With Mrs. Matthews in her corner, maybe there was hope for her and Jack.

They had never felt the need for constant talk during their times together, but Jack's morose attitude on the ride to Wellsburg made her uncomfortable. Never had she felt his emotional wall so forbidding. She understood his concern for his niece, but she couldn't get him to talk about work, the weather, or even Blythe. She almost asked him why he had bothered to invite her along. She could have driven herself. After an almost silent ride, they walked into the hospital room and greeted Mark.

Jack laid his hand on Mark's shoulder. "How are you, Bro'?"

The dark circles under Mark's eyes and the lines on his face declared his stress. "I'm glad you're here."

Tears flooded Kate's eyes. The little girl lay with the oxygen mask over her mouth and nose and was connected to an IV and monitors which beeped periodically. Blythe opened her eyes just long enough to acknowledge their presence. Kate's eyes sought Jack's tear-filled ones then Mark's. She fought the rising lump in her throat.

"She's susceptible to respiratory trouble, like her mother. I thought she had a cold. I didn't see this coming," Mark said, tiredness lacing his speech. He raked his fingers through his hair. "Blythe's been asking for you, Kate. Thank you for coming."

Kate laid her hand on Mark's arm and squeezed, unable to speak.

Mark's fatigued face broke into a grin. He nudged his brother. "You know, Jack, she's one in a million. Don't let her get away."

She caught Jack's eye, but he looked away quickly. Kate saw his frown, however, and she turned back toward Blythe to hide her hurt. "Mrs. Matthews wanted me to assure you that she and Mr. Matthews are praying for all of you."

"Mr. and Mrs. Matthews are true prayer warriors. In spite of the fact that she is a busybody," Mark added, catching Jack's eye, "she has a heart of gold."

Kate didn't know why Jack stepped over to stand beside her as she watched Blythe. She didn't trust her voice, but she wished he would say something to diffuse the tension between them. She wanted him to affirm that she was special to him. That he wouldn't let her get away. He either wouldn't or couldn't say the words. And this wasn't the time or place to pursue the issue.

"Jack," she said finally, "why don't you take Mark to get something to eat? I'll stay here with Blythe. Mark needs a break." And she needed to be alone.

Jack's tight expression relaxed. "Good idea. How about some food, Mark?"

"I think I could use the break, as long as you don't mind,

Kate. I had a slice of toast and a cup of coffee early this morning, but I'm ready for more food."

"We'll bring you something, Kate," Jack added, and the brothers exited the room.

Kate blew out a deep breath when they left. As she sat in a chair next to Blythe's bed, she wanted to pull the little girl to her and will her to be well. Instead she bowed her head and prayed. "Please, Father, make Blythe well again. I don't know what I'd do if I lost her. I can only imagine what Mark is feeling right now. Please help Mark and Jack, because they both love her so much. Help them to trust You. Please help Blythe, Father. Make her body strong again. In Jesus' name, amen."

Kate pulled a tissue from her purse to wipe tears from her eyes and cheeks and blow her nose. Blythe opened her eyes again. Kate gently laid her hand on the hot hand of her little friend. "Hi, sweetie, I hope you get better soon. I miss you."

Blythe's eyes closed. Kate began to softly sing Blythe's favorite Sunday school songs. A nurse came in to check the little girl. She smiled at Kate. "Her temperature is down and her color is better." The nurse entered information into her computer.

Kate nodded. "That's good." Mark and Jack would be glad to know that. After the nurse left the room, she whispered, "Thank you, Father God."

During the quiet ride back to Millvale, Kate reached over and touched Jack's hand on the stick shift. "She'll get better."

His jaw tightened. He grabbed her fingers. "I hope so," was all he said.

She should have insisted that he let her drive home. He drove carefully enough, but she could see he struggled to keep his emotions in check. First his parents, then Mark's wife, and now Blythe. Her heart ached for him.

They stopped at the diner for coffee and pie, taking seats that allowed them to see the ducks on the Mill Pond. They ate quietly. Kate missed Blythe's running commentary on the ducks.

While they ate, Kate wondered how to comfort Jack, how to break through the wall of silence.

He broke the silence. "It's so hard to see Blythe like that, like her mother, before she died." His voice wobbled.

She looked up, surprised that he spoke. "Did Rachael have pneumonia often?"

"Every year. Why do people we love have to die and leave us, Kate?" A sob escaped his throat. Kate waited, not sure he expected an answer. He continued. "Mom and Dad lived their faith. They taught us about God's love and care. Mom gave up a career to raise Mark and me. Dad was a pilot, so he had to be away a lot." He shook his head. "It's ironic they died in a plane crash, on a trip together. I never understood why God allowed them to die and leave us."

Kate swallowed around the lump in her throat. "I don't know, Jack. I wondered that after Tim died. It's the way life is. We expect old people to die, so it's not so hard to accept. But children and younger adults . . ." Kate pressed her fork into pie crumbs on her plate. "Knowing Tim's in heaven helps a lot. Blythe told me her mommy taught her about how Jesus died for her sins, and she asked Him to be her Savior."

He stared out the window. "It's just too hard, Kate, to love someone and then lose her. Maybe it would be easier not to care."

"You don't really believe that, do you, Jack?" He didn't answer or look at her. Her hopes sank. She watched the ducks outside the window. The mother duck scolded, and a black and yellow duckling put his head underwater. She thought about Mr. and Mrs. Matthews' fifty-year marriage and her own parents. She thought about Tim and the love they had shared. The world would be a darker place if Blythe had never been born.

Jack was mistaken. Love was worth the pain of separation. She wanted to hold him by the shoulders and shake him until he believed.

In a voice just above a whisper she said, "When Tim died, at first I couldn't believe it. I kept waiting for him to knock on the door or call me on the phone. I didn't want to go on without him. People tried to comfort me, but I didn't want their comfort. I was so angry that he died and left me behind, so angry at God for letting him die. That's when Ellie asked me to work for her, and I came to Millvale. To escape the pain and loss. To escape memories of Tim. In time, the good memories became stronger, and the sense of loss not as painful. God gave me the strength to go on. I began to paint again, and then I met Blythe."

Jack said nothing, only stared out the window, but she knew he was listening. Clearing her throat, she continued. "Blythe is still with us, Jack. She's still alive. She's in God's care, and there's no better place for her."

Jack pulled his napkin from his lap, crumpled it, and threw it on the table. He stood and held out his hand. "It's time for the evening service. Mark wants me to let people at church know how Blythe is doing."

She stood without taking his hand. He picked up the check, left a tip, and paid for their food on the way out.

WHEN BLYTHE RETURNED to painting class a week later, she reminded Kate of fragile china. Blue veins showed through translucent skin. Her brown eyes seemed larger than normal in her thin face.

Mark's pale face and the dark circles under his eyes gave witness to the strain he felt.

"She insisted she had to come back to class today. She didn't want you and her friends to worry about her, and she didn't want to miss painting class again. I'll be nearby, so don't hesitate to call me if there's a problem."

Kate laid her hand on the man's arm. "I'll take good care of her, Mark. Painting doesn't take a lot of physical activity, and she loves it, so maybe it's the best thing for her."

He patted her hand and left.

"I had 'monia," the little girl informed her interested classmates. "God made me better."

Painting class ended with the month of July. Business at the shop slowed, and the next big event was Ellie's wedding. Kate anticipated having more time for painting and Blythe. She wasn't sure about Jack. As the girl took on a healthier glow, and her normal energy level started to return, Kate sighed with relief. Thinking back to the beautiful spring afternoon when she had met Blythe, she now understood the air of fragility about the child she had noticed when they first met.

A shadow of uneasiness, like a premonition, settled over her.

CHAPTER FIVE

On the evening of August 1, Kate's cell phone rang as she turned the key to open her apartment door. She struggled through the doorway with her bags of groceries, willing the phone to keep ringing until she could pull it from her pocket and answer it.

Her parents' number. Probably her mother. She answered, trying to catch her breath. "Hello."

"Hello, Katie." Her father's voice sounded tense.

"Dad? Is that you? Is something wrong?"

"Yes, there is." Kate held her breath as her father continued. "Can you come home? I—We need your help." His voice broke.

Alarm tightened her chest. "Why? What's the matter?" Kate knew her father didn't cry often.

"Your mother. She has breast cancer."

Her breath caught as if someone had punched her in the gut. "Oh, Dad! I'm so sorry."

Her father paused and then said, "Will you come?"

"When? How long . . .?"

"What I'm asking, is that you move back home for a while. Your mother needs someone here with her. If it were just a week or two, I might be able to do it myself. But I have to run the business. I have good employees, but I'm the owner."

"But, Dad, I have a job and—"

"I know, Katie. Your mother asked me to call you. She wants you to come home."

She panicked. "What about Kevin?" She planned to visit soon, so why did her father's request scare her so?

"Your brother has his family to think about and can't get away right now. I know this is hard for you. If you can't, I'll do what I have to do. Will you at least think about it? Please?"

Guilt washed over her because she had made her father beg. "I can't come until after Ellie's wedding. I'm a bridesmaid, and I have to take care of the shop while she's on her honeymoon. Is that okay?"

Kate's father released a huge sigh. "That will be fine. You'll never know how much this means to us. Your mom misses you. She'll be so happy to have you home."

He didn't say he missed her, but she knew he meant it. "I know, Dad."

"I can keep the business going and make sure the bills are paid. I'll be home every weekend, so you'll have some free time. And we'll pay you."

"That won't be necessary." She'd been self-supporting for over a year. That her parents offered to pay her irked and embarrassed her. "Will Mom have to have surgery or chemo?" Kate squeaked past the lump in her throat.

"The surgery is scheduled for next week, a mastectomy, and then she'll have chemotherapy. You should be home by the time that starts." Kate recognized the forced cheerfulness in his voice. Or maybe it was hope. "They're making a lot of progress with cancer cures nowadays, you know."

"So I've heard. I'm so sorry, Dad. Tell Mom I love her." She swallowed a sob. "I'll call you back either tomorrow or the next day to check on Mom and to let you know when I'll be there."

"Sure, Katie. Thanks. We really do miss you."

"I know. I miss you too. And I'll see you soon." She ended the call and dropped the phone in her lap.

Kate sat on the sofa and sobbed. The pink glow of the sunset through the window belied the pain in her heart. Ready or not, she would return to Mountain View at the end of August. Her mind in a whirl, her feelings conflicted, Kate stifled the urge to call Jack, uncertain of his reaction, not ready to talk to anyone else. She'd wait until morning to tell Ellie.

MARK TOOK his daughter to her doctor's appointments and stayed close to home for the present, so Jack didn't come around as often. Back-to-school sales had kept him at work for longer hours as well. Kate didn't know when or if she'd see him again. She tried not to think about it. On Sunday morning, he surprised her when he knocked on her door.

When she opened the apartment door, he took one look at her and said, "Is something wrong?" He stepped in, leaving the door ajar.

Kate knew from her reflection in the mirror that morning that she looked as exhausted as she felt. Dark shadows underlined her eyes. She nodded. "My mom . . . my mother has cancer. I have to go home."

Tears flowed, and Jack put his arms around her and held her until she gained control.

His arms gave her comfort. She closed her eyes and leaned into his embrace.

"I'm sorry. Why didn't you call me?" He brushed her hair away from her cheek.

She wanted to cry out, "Because I didn't know if you would care!" Instead she said, "I knew you were putting in extra time at work, so I didn't want to bother you." Kate had confided only in

Ellie, with the condition not to tell anyone except Ben. She needed the time to process the information before making it public.

"It wouldn't have been a bother. That's what friends are for."

Friends? She knew that was true, but she wanted more. She wanted to share her heart, and even her life, with him, but did he care enough? She pushed herself away and grabbed a tissue from the small table near the door, along with her purse and Bible. She had her parents to consider now.

"I'm okay. We'd better go, or we'll be late for church." She said and slipped past him.

He nodded as his eyes followed her. He pulled the door closed behind them.

Today, Kate didn't shut herself away. She let the love of her friends refresh her, like dry ground receiving the soaking rain. She couldn't count the number of people who came up to her with words of comfort and promises to pray for her mother and her family. She left church hopeful, except in her relationship with Jack.

Unless they had an invitation to eat with friends, Kate and Jack ate at Mill Pond Diner after church on Sundays. This week, because of Blythe's recent illness, Mark remained at home with his daughter. Kate and Jack ate alone together. Although she loved Blythe, she preferred this time alone with him today.

As usual, after the meal, the couple sat beside the Mill Pond, watching the ducks. They laughed over the antics of the duck-lings, now nearly as large as their mother. The quacking, flapping, and dunking distracted Kate from melancholy thoughts, making her smile.

Jack laughed at a young duck going through a voice change. Its peep suddenly changed into a squawk. "Have you noticed that the boy ducks aren't as loud as the girl ducks?" Jack asked with a teasing glint.

Kate poked her companion gently with her elbow. "The

mothers have to be louder, because they are responsible for the ducklings. They have to make sure their children hear them."

The ducks waded out of the pond and settled to rest on the bank, amid quiet duck chattering and mild quacking. Kate wondered if ducks shared secrets. She found herself without words. She would miss this. She would miss Millvale.

Jack looked repeatedly at Kate as though waiting for her to say something. He finally broke the silence. "How long will you be gone?"

"I don't know." She brushed a wrinkle out of her skirt, crossed her ankles, and clasped her hands in her lap. "I don't know how long Mom's treatments will last, and I don't know how long she'll need me. She'll begin chemotherapy after she has time to heal from the surgery."

"Do you know when you are going? Have you set a date when you'll leave Millvale?"

Kate stood and took a couple of steps away from him toward the pond. "I told Ellie I'd wait until after her honeymoon." Her conscience goaded her about not returning to Mountain View for her mother's surgery, even though Mom urged her to wait. "My mom said not to worry. Her friends, Myra and Jill, will fill in the gap until I get there. Kevin will be there with Dad during her surgery." She turned back toward Jack. "I'll leave the day after Ellie and Ben return."

Jack folded his arms and leaned forward, looking at the ground. "Are you coming back?"

Kate didn't respond right away. She gazed across the pond, her eyes resting on the green hill beyond. "I don't know. Maybe not. I don't know what's going to happen, whether my mom will make it." She choked up on the last phrase.

"Blythe will miss you. I'm sure Ellie will too."

What about Jack? Didn't he realize how much he could influence her decision? She waited for him to ask her to return, saying he needed her to come back.

He looked up. "I . . ." He bit his lip with a slight shake of his head and looked away.

Maybe he really didn't want her here.

THE WHIRLWIND OF WEDDING PREPARATIONS, a bridal shower, and talking shop with Ellie helped to ease the pain of coming separation and thoughts of her mother's illness. Although she shed many private tears, Kate had no intention of dampening her friend's joy and wedding celebration with her own problems. She carried a smile on her face and a heavy weight on her chest. She prayed for the ability to forget about herself.

Mark asked Kate to take Blythe shopping to choose a dress to wear to the wedding. "I don't know what Blythe will do when you leave, Kate. You have been so good for her. She needs a mother, but I'm not ready to get married again." They stood outside Mill Valley Florist just after Kate closed for the day.

"Don't rush yourself, Mark. I'm no expert, but I don't think you should remarry just to give Blythe a mother. You loved Rachael very much, and one day you will love again. We have both been blessed to find true love once."

Kate wondered why, even though they both loved Blythe and they had both lost someone they loved, she never felt more than a sisterly affection for Mark.

"Do you think you'll come back to Millvale?" he asked, breaking into her thoughts.

"I don't know. It depends on several things."

"If that thick-skulled brother of mine doesn't smarten up."

"Evidently God has something else planned for me and for Jack. I'm going to continue painting, and I hope to sell my work. I'd like to get married and have a big family, but that may not be for me. At least right now." Her brave words didn't ease her aching heart.

They walked toward Kate's car. "You know, Kate, Jack and I both struggled after our parents died. When Rachael died, he lost a big sister. They were close." He crossed his fingers. "Her death devastated both of us. And you, he knows you lost Tim. My brother chooses to hold back rather than lose someone else he loves." Mark laid his hand on Kate's shoulder. "I think you're wise to move forward with your life and plans. But be patient, Kate. He'll come around. Once he finally makes up his mind, he won't change it again."

She chose not to voice her doubts about Jack. Mark understood his brother and knew how she felt about him. She arranged to take Blythe shopping the following evening, knowing it would be an adventure and a welcome distraction for her to help the little girl choose the perfect dress.

Blythe's loving hugs and cheerful chatter helped Kate as they shopped. After two hours and three stores, they found the right dress, sandals, and hair bow for the occasion. On the way home, Blythe agreed they should finish their "girls' night out" with milkshakes at the diner. They giggled together at Kate's cell phone photos of Blythe posing "like a real model" in several dresses she had tried on, and at double-selfies of them making faces. When they settled down to sip their shakes, Kate's mind returned to the uncertainties she faced. Would her mother survive cancer? Would she ever return to Millvale? What about Jack? The ups and downs of their relationship made her feel like a yo-yo in his hands.

She slid her cup back and forth in front of her as she responded absently to the child's chatter. A soft hand touched her cheek, "Don't be sad, Kate. Jesus made me better. I'm praying for your mother. I know she'll get better too."

Kate laid her hand on Blythe's head and smiled at her, touched by the child's sensitivity.

"You're right, Blythe. Jesus is taking care of my mother. Thank you for reminding me."

Fretting over the future had not helped her in the past. She struggled to convince her heart what her mind knew. God would fit these broken pieces into His master plan for her.

Please help me, Father God. What am I to do? I thought Jack might be the one, but I'm not sure. I wish he would say something, tell me how he feels. Help me remember You know and want the best for me and for Jack. It's so hard to let go.

JACK HAD AVOIDED COMING to Millvale since Sunday. He even excused himself from attending the Wednesday evening service by saying he had to work overtime at Clint's Computers. He came on Thursday to stay with Blythe while Mark went out of town for business overnight. He wished he hadn't.

"You have to make your own decision, but I am going to give my opinion. You'll be a fool to let Kate go. At least tell her how you feel." Mark put up his hand when Jack started to protest. "Don't make excuses. It's obvious how you really feel about her. I've never seen you look at a woman the way you look at her, nor have you ever spent as much time with anyone. It's obvious she loves you." Mark looked at his brother with a half-smile. "Maybe it's time you took your niece's advice."

Jack, fighting angry words he wanted to spit out at his interfering brother, simply said, "That's right, it's my decision!"

He took Mark's words seriously, however. Five years his senior, his big brother had tried to be brother and father to the young teen after their parents' untimely death. A great uncle had come to live with them for a few years, until the old man died, so the boys could remain together.

Mark's love and steadiness had helped Jack through that difficult time. Mark's opinion mattered.

He took a deep breath and nodded. "I'll think about it."

A FEW DAYS LATER, Kate and Ellie shared a last lunch out before the wedding. "We've done a good job, if I say so myself." Ellie reached around and patted her own back.

Kate held out her hand. "We make a good team." They shook hands.

Ellie stirred her iced tea with a straw. "What do you think of the idea of becoming wedding planners? We could start a business together."

Ellie's direct look and half-smile showed that she was serious. Kate shook her head. "No, Ellie. Although going into business with you wouldn't be a problem, I want to earn my living by painting. I wouldn't have time for both. I lost one dream when Tim died, but I still have my painting."

"Uh-huh. Going into business with me would keep you from that dream. I understand." She smiled. "But we could have lots of fun together."

Kate leaned forward. "You are a wonderful friend, Ellie. You helped me get on with my life when I felt so crushed that I didn't think I had a future. You were God's gift to me at a time when I felt I had nothing left." She took her friend's hand. "Thank you."

"Oh, Katie, you should be ashamed, making me cry in public!" She pulled a napkin from the table dispenser. "Is my mascara running?" When Kate shook her head, Ellie continued. "You have been a stellar employee. I'll never be able to replace you. You know your job will be here when you come back."

"I don't think I'll be back." Kate leaned back in her chair. Her fingers tapped a rhythm on the table top.

Ellie raised her eyebrows. "Why? You've told me many times that this is your home."

"Yes, but sometimes things change. There are circumstances out of my control."

"You mean Jack?"

Kate took a sip of iced tea. "He's one reason. I feel like our relationship goes forward two steps and back two steps. I love Jack, but I don't think he wants to be more than just friends."

"What do you think is holding him back?"

"He has lost so many people he loves, he wonders if it's worthwhile to love at all."

"He really said that?"

"Yes, during Blythe's last illness, when we went to the hospital. I won't try to force him into a relationship he doesn't believe in."

"I'm sorry, Kate. Have you told him how you feel?"

"Not directly. I'm just old-fashioned and a little afraid. I think he needs to say it first. Every time we start drawing closer, he puts up his wall of resistance. Besides, now I'm leaving Millvale."

Ellie leaned forward, and Kate expected a lecture. Instead Ellie sighed and said, "I wish things could be different. I think you two could have a good life together."

"That may be true. But for now, I'm going to focus on helping Mom get better and improving my painting. After your honeymoon, of course. Do you know where you're going?"

They launched into a discussion of honeymoon plans and final wedding details. Kate wished she could turn off thoughts about her own love life as they talked about Ellie and Ben's plans.

CHAPTER SIX

The Somers family arrived in Millvale in time for Alana, Ellie's sister, to have a fitting for her gown. From distant Africa, Alana had agreed to the choice of jade satin in a similar style to the bride's gown. She was quite pleased with the fit, color, and style when she tried it on.

At Kate's invitation, Alana slept at her apartment. Kate made up a bed on the floor so Alana could sleep on the sofa. Not having seen each other since Tim's funeral, the two young women stayed up late several nights, sharing memories of college days and catching up on each other's lives.

"You'll have another chance at marriage soon, Katie. I see you have a beau."

Kate frowned. "Huh! You and Ellie are hopeless matchmakers." She relaxed her expression. "What about you, Alana? What's happening in your life?"

"Uh-uh. Don't change the subject. I know Jack. We grew up together. I've seen how he looks at you."

"I don't think he wants any more than friendship."

"Have you told him how you feel?"

Kate held out her hands. "Jack has lost a lot of people in his life and is afraid to commit to a serious relationship. He's my friend. That's it for now. I'll be leaving soon anyway." Kate put up her hand when Alana began to protest. "There's nothing more to say. I'm tired of feeling like an emotional yo-yo. Now, tell me about your work."

Alana worked for an international aid agency that went into Third World countries. Her work in the past year had involved administering care to people suffering from war, drought, and famine. She shared a photo album and experiences with her friend.

"I don't know how you do it, Lanie. Isn't it hard to see so much suffering?" Kate stopped at a page with photographs of children with protruding ribs.

Alana bit her lip thoughtfully before answering. "Yes, it often is. We don't realize how much people around the world suffer, from diseases that can be helped by immunizations or better hygiene. War makes it so much worse. The children are the hardest to see." Alana's voice broke. Kate reached for a box of tissues, and her friend continued. "I try to focus on the ones I can help. I do have opportunities to share my faith, though I have to be careful how I do it and when." She paused a moment. "We hear so much about the tragedies, but successes are often ignored. Maybe I'll write a book about our work, to encourage people to keep helping, to keep trying." Kate handed her a tissue. She wiped her eyes and sniffed.

"You may not be able to say the words out loud, but when you help the people, I think you share your faith more eloquently than with words."

"I hope so. Thanks, friend." Alana blew her nose.

KATE APPRECIATED Alana's help in the shop for a couple of days before the wedding. She had never seen Ellie so distracted. Kate took the responsibility of getting the flowers ready for the church and reception, as well as the wedding party. Ellie had chosen pale pink as an accent to the jade. The beautiful but simple arrangements were more in keeping with Ellie and Ben's expense account than what had been used for the Smith wedding earlier in the summer.

The day dawned warm and bright. Kate began it truly happy for her friends. This was the culmination of her year in Millvale, a day filled with memorable moments and beauty and a few humorous glitches. The bride misplaced her sandals, and they had to scramble to find them. The flower girl sat down on the floor to play with the rose petals in her basket, and Pastor Clary faltered over the groom's name at the end of the ceremony.

At the reception, Blythe twirled and flitted from person to person in her blue dress with pink rose buds. She often returned to Kate, holding her hand or giving her a hug.

"I think Blythe thinks she's the hostess. She hasn't missed a person," Jack said, smiling at Kate. "She calls it her 'princess dress.' You helped her pick it out, she told me." Kate nearly stopped breathing when he took her hand and added, "You look beautiful today."

She couldn't look away. She knew he loved her. Would he say what she longed to hear? Weddings had a way of giving you a different perspective on life. Had he realized that he didn't have to let past losses prevent a committed and successful marriage for them?

"Thank you, Jack," she whispered, on the verge of tears. Her emotions on edge from the wedding and her pending departure from Millvale, she almost wished Jack hadn't spoken those words to her in that tone of voice and gazed at her with those blue eyes. She searched for the right words to say, her heart filled with too many things she'd like to say. She brushed an imaginary wrinkle from the skirt of her dress.

He pressed her hand between both of his own. "Katie, I need to tell you . . ."

"Kate!" Ellie called to her from across the reception hall, motioning with her hand.

If Ellie had only waited. "Okay," she answered. "Be right there." She stepped back. Jack's face invited her to stay. She wanted to stay. "I have to go. The bride calls." She trembled as she turned away.

He let go of her hand and stuffed his hands in his pockets. "Okay, I'll talk to you later."

She glanced back to see him watching her. He looked so handsome in his gray suit, blue shirt, and tie. Her heart sank as he shook his head and turned away with a frown on his face.

She became so busy helping Ellie, posing for photographs, and talking to guests, she saw him only from across the room after that. She watched him eating cake, laughing with Blythe, and talking to other wedding guests, but never looking her way. After the bride and groom had left, she looked around for him.

No Jack.

She supposed she couldn't blame him for leaving. They hadn't come as a couple. But she wished he had waited. Sighing, she couldn't throw off the sense of loss.

KATE COULDN'T REMEMBER many details from her last week in Millvale. Jack's emotional distance caused her feelings for him to shift from longing, to hurt, to anger. With few customers at Mill Valley Florist, she used the time to clean and organize. Ellie would have plenty to do when she returned. Fall stock would be in soon. Alana, who remained in Millvale for part of the week, helped her. Kate appreciated her friend's presence, mostly for the companionship. Alana left on Thursday, Ellie returned on Friday, and Kate prepared to leave the next day.

They stood in the driveway of Ellie's new home. The morning sun reflected off the house, but dark clouds peaked over the western horizon.

"I'm sorry you have to go, Katie." Ellie gave her a long hug. "I hope your mom gets better soon. Remember, your job will be here if and when you come back."

Kate clung to her friend. "Thank you, Ellie. Your wedding was beautiful, and I'm glad you let me be a part. Be happy. Let's be sure to keep in touch."

She said goodbye to Ben and got into her car. She would miss her friends.

The Chambers' cottage was the last stop for Kate on her way out of Millvale. Blythe came rushing down the front steps toward her and threw herself at Kate. She held on as though she'd never let go. Her big, brown eyes filled with tears. Jack, there to care for his niece, followed more slowly.

"Kate, why do you have to go?" the little girl sobbed.

Kate kneeled in front of Blythe and took both of her hands. "You know. I told you my mother is sick and needs me to take care of her."

"Why can't she move here and live in your apartment?"

Kate smiled. "Mountain View is her home. It's better for her to stay home and for me to go there." She brushed Blythe's hair back from her tear-stained face.

Blythe sniffed. "But I want you to stay! You'll come back, won't you?" Blythe hugged her again. "I'm going to miss you. I want your mother to get better, but I'm going to pray Jesus makes her better real fast. Then you can come back."

"I'll miss you too, sweetie. I'll try to come back to see you. We'll write, okay?" When Blythe nodded, she continued. "Send me pictures. Maybe your daddy will let you e-mail me."

Kate handed a paper to Blythe. "Here's my address in Mountain View and my e-mail." She glanced up at Jack, who stood a few steps away, watching them.

Blythe clutched the paper. "I'm going to paint a picture just for you. I'm going to be a good artist, just like you."

Kate laughed and hugged her again. "Keep practicing. Maybe you'll be better than me."

Blythe put her lips to Kate's ear and whispered, "I want you to marry Uncle Jack."

"Oh, Blythe," Kate said softly. *So do I.* She looked up and caught Jack's gaze. "Why don't you go put the paper in a safe place?"

Blythe ran into the cottage, clutching the precious paper. Kate stood and brushed off the legs of her jeans. She looked around the flower-filled yard and swallowed hard.

Jack, his hands in his pockets, scuffed the toe of his sneaker in the grass. She wished she could read his thoughts. Or maybe not.

"So, how is your mother doing?"

"She has been scheduled to begin chemotherapy next week. She seems up-beat."

He searched her face. "I'll miss you, Kate."

"Will you, Jack?" Her gaze held his, unsmiling, challenging him.

He stepped toward her. "Of course. Did you doubt that?" Jack's hands grasped her shoulders, and he lowered his mouth to her lips. As though surprised by his own action, he stepped back quickly, and shook his head. "You understand, don't you, Kate? I can't take the chance. Being friends has to be enough."

The kiss surprised her. Kate's lips tingled, and she ran her tongue over them. "No, Jack, I don't understand. I have good reason to doubt that you really care. After all these months." Kate choked up. "You . . . I thought . . ."

"At the wedding I thought I wanted to talk, but it's too hard, Kate, too hard to love someone and lose her. You should understand. Look at my brother. Look at you and Tim. And Blythe." Jack's voice broke, and he shook his head. "I can't."

Blythe stood on the front steps watching them, so Kate wouldn't have chosen this time to discuss their relationship. But with time running out, she turned her back to Blythe and spoke her mind.

"You're wrong, Jack. Relationships take effort and faith. You don't believe that God could bless our relationship. I've never regretted my relationship with Tim. I've never regretted loving him. And I'll never regret loving . . ." She wanted to add "you."

Jack looked down, stuffing his hands in his pockets. He wouldn't say the words he knew she wanted to hear from his lips. He shook his head. "I have to be honest with you."

Kate took a deep breath and stepped back. "So, this is good-bye? This is the end?" Feeling limp and no longer able to argue, she said, "You'll be a lonely man, Jack Chambers. Some day you won't even have memories!" Kate choked back a sob.

Jack looked up. "Kate, I . . ."

Kate waited, but he said no more. He cast his eyes down and dug a hole in the ground with the toe of his shoe.

Angry and regretful tears filled her eyes. She snapped. "I'm tired of your games, Jack, tired of being dangled like a yo-yo!"

Jack stood with his mouth open at her angry outburst. Although immediately sorry for her sharp words, she refused to apologize. She strode to her car. She shook her head as she slid into her seat, started the car, and drove away from Millvale and Jack.

CHAPTER SEVEN

Jack couldn't believe it. Kate, gone! He didn't want her to leave angry. He didn't want her to go. He wanted to assure her that he would always be there for her. The words refused to come out. He hadn't tried to stop her as he watched her get into her car and drive away.

One day later he couldn't believe how much he missed her already, what a void her leaving Millvale had left in his heart and in his life. Surely he would get over her, and the empty feeling would pass.

He regretted that he had hurt her. The comment about the yo-yo. Did he really do that to her? He had never made any promises. After all, he wasn't a marrying sort of guy. He couldn't stand the thought of the kind of commitment that could bring such pain. She should understand that.

He wasn't prepared for the ache in his heart at her absence. Jack assumed Kate would stick around for a long time. Her leaving had been a shock, although not enough of a shock for him to change his mind about marriage. Every time he passed Mill Valley Florist, he expected her Honda to be parked out front. He hoped to see her sitting with Blythe when he walked into church, and he waited for her to come through the door of Mill Pond Diner. Sometimes he heard her voice or laughter in a crowd.

Blythe kept him updated, sharing Kate's letters and emails with her uncle.

"Uncle Jack, look, I got a letter from Kate. She drew me a picture too."

"That's nice, princess." Jack pretended nonchalance.

"You wanna read it?"

"Sure, if you want me to." He tried to read between the lines of Kate's letters to his niece, but the simple words gave away no secrets.

He could call Kate. He knew her cell phone number. He stubbornly refused. She had left hurt, but he couldn't help her. He had never made her any promises. She wanted something from him that he couldn't give her. He wasn't being selfish, just honest. He would have to learn to forget her.

That was easier said than done. An image of the pretty young woman with blue-green eyes and honey-blonde hair remained cemented in his brain and heart.

The hardest place to be was the meadow, their playground with Blythe. The song of the wind through the blue spruce whispered her name. He pictured her seated at the picnic table or on the swing attached to a hefty branch. Kate had spent hours sketching and painting at the meadow. She had called it her studio.

Blythe, in first grade now, remained healthy and excelled in her studies. Both men knew she missed Kate. The young woman had become an important part of the little girl's life, filling in some of the empty places left by her mother's death. Blythe always looked for a letter from Kate, or she asked to be allowed to check for a message from Kate on email when she got home after school. Sometimes she watched out the window as though waiting for Kate's blue car to pull up in their driveway. More than once, at the picnic table in the meadow, Blythe sat with her chin resting on her flattened fingers, looking across the meadow with unseeing eyes.

"Are you all right, Princess?" he asked one cloudy autumn day.

Blythe twisted her mouth. "Yes, Uncle Jack. I'm okay. When do you think Kate will be back?" She played with the edge of her drawing pad and her colored pencils.

"Kate has to take care of her mother. She won't come back until her mother is better."

"When Kate comes back, are you going to marry her?"

The sadness in her eyes wrenched his heart. "I'm not planning to. I'm trying to get my business started."

Blythe studied Jack's face. "Can't you start your business and marry Kate?"

How do you explain to a six-going-on-seven-year-old the intricacies of relationships? Her question stumped him, especially since he struggled with the thought of his own irrationality in the matter. He shrugged. "I think I'll concentrate on my new business for now."

"Oh, okay," she responded sadly. "I hope she comes back soon anyway."

BEGINNING the process of setting up his own business helped him take his mind off Kate, sometimes. The blooming of goldenrod and purple asters, and the changing colors of the leaves on the sugar maples made him wish she were here to paint them.

He figured he'd be ready to open his own store in about six months. He had saved up some money and looked into getting a small business loan. Hours of Internet research gave him information he needed to set up his business. He checked into some courses at the community college as well. He asked his brother for advice, and he told Ben and Ellie his plans. Talking to Ellie made him feel closer to Kate, although he would have denied it if asked. He began to look around Millvale for an appropriate location to set up his business.

"What do you think, Mark? Should I look for a place to rent on Main Street, or should I look for a place to buy where I could have a shop and an apartment to live in?"

Mark sat back in his chair and looked at his brother thoughtfully. They were having lunch together at the cottage. Mark would be leaving on business the next morning, so Jack had come to stay with Blythe. He had taken a personal day off from his job to look at available real estate in Millvale.

As they sat across the table from each other, with Mark staring at him, Jack wondered if his brother would ask him the same question Blythe had asked: was he going to marry Kate? Or tell him to stop being irrational. Jack knew he had disappointed his big brother, whose good opinion mattered so much to him. Although they had some distant relatives, cousins or something, on the other side of the country, he and Mark and Blythe had only each other. They were family. Now Jack had given Mark a good opening to rake him over the coals.

"I guess that all depends." Mark leaned forward, resting his elbows on the table. He steepled his fingers and looked at Jack over them. "Can you tell me what you've discovered? I know you're looking at real estate today. And I know you've been researching this for a while."

Jack heaved a sigh of relief and launched into a summary of his plans and what he had discovered, encouraged each time Mark nodded. Talking about it made him even more excited about the possibility of opening his own store.

"Have you checked at the real estate office? They might have some listings you're not aware of."

Jack shifted in his chair. "I looked around this morning, and

I've checked listings on-line. But I'm hoping you'll go to the real estate office with me this afternoon."

Mark raised his eyebrows. "You can't go by yourself?"

"Well, I could, but I thought your input would be helpful."

"And . . ."

Jack ran his hand across the back of his neck. His brother knew him too well. "Mary Jo King works there. She's pushy."

Mark gestured with his hand. "She's a salesperson. That's how she sells properties."

"I don't mean that way. She's single, and since Kate left, she practically throws herself at me." The heat rose up his neck and into his face at this confession.

Mark chuckled. "Oh, she did have a big crush on you in high school, didn't she? Well, she's not bad-looking, and she is a believer. Is that really so bad?"

"Mark, I can't make her believe I'm not interested, and I don't want to be totally rude. She's good at her job, though. I thought you would help me out. Maybe she won't be so aggressive if you're there."

Mark smiled. "Sure. Want to go right after we clean up here? That way I can be home when Blythe gets out of school."

Jack sighed with relief. "Okay. I'll load the dishwasher while you put away the food."

On the way to town in Jack's car, Mark spoke. "Have you thought about a logo for your business?"

Jack shrugged. "I've tried, but I'm not very creative. I want something simple and defining, so people don't have to wonder what kind of business I run. I want a logo that shouts, 'That's Jack Chamber's computer business!'"

Mark laughed at his brother's enthusiasm. "Have you thought of asking Kate Greenway to create one for you?"

Jack snapped back, "It's over between us. Don't try to force us back together!" He didn't like that the mention of Kate's name left him feeling so vulnerable.

Mark put up his hand. "Cool down, Jack. Kate's an artist, and you know she does good work. I thought you might like to encourage her in her career."

Jack took a deep breath. "Okay. I'm sorry I jumped at you." He stopped at a crosswalk to let a pedestrian cross. "She's not a graphic artist. I don't know if she would want to do it."

"Why don't you ask her?"

"I haven't heard from Kate since she left in August."

"You could open the line of communication."

"I know." Jack paused as he parked in front of Valley Real Estate. "I've thought about it, but I don't want to give her any false hope about a relationship with me."

"Kate's not going to force you into anything. She has proven that she won't push you, though she obviously cares for you. She's not like Mary Jo."

Jack tapped on the steering wheel. "Blythe misses her. I've been thinking, maybe after Christmas she and I could take a ride to Mountain View."

"Why not now?"

"I'm not ready yet. By then I'll have more definite plans for the business, and I'll know what I want for a logo. I'll have more vacation time then as well." True, Jack wasn't ready, but not because of business plans or vacation time. He wasn't ready to face Kate yet. He feared being rejected by her, and he feared his attraction for her.

The brothers got out of the car and headed into the real estate office.

"I'm with you, Brother," Mark said, clapping Jack's shoulder. "Let's go talk with Mary Jo King."

CHAPTER EIGHT

For the first weeks after returning to her parents' home in Mountain View, Kate gratefully accepted the busyness. Her mother's surgery went well, but the chemotherapy made her ill and frail. Kate took her to her treatments, nursed her during the day, and often stayed up with her at night.

When her mother's beautiful, thick hair fell out in globs, she held the older woman and cried with her. Together they chose a wig and several hats for her mother to wear.

"You are our life preserver, Katie," her father confided. She considered herself a deflated one.

From childhood, her passion had been painting, and she dreamed of making a living as an artist. Recently, going to her studio in her parents' basement brought comfort and relief from the frustration that came with having to move back with her parents and taking care of her sick mother. The smell of paint, the motion of her brush strokes as she applied the colors to paper or canvas, and seeing her paintings come to life soothed her soul and her creative spirit.

God had thrown her other lifelines as well: His Word, prayer, and church.

"You need to go to church, Katie," her father urged. "I'm here with your mother."

Kate heeded her father's urging and went to church. In fact, she looked forward to it, renewing former friendships and making new friends. Surrounded by her Christian community as she sang songs of praise and listened to the preaching, she was comforted and encouraged, not like after Tim's death, when her shattered hopes and dreams made her want to get away from everything that reminded her of Tim and from the God who had allowed him to die.

Kate looked forward to receiving Blythe's weekly letters, each one accompanied by a delightful drawing. She composed a picture storybook about the little girl's beloved meadow as her Christmas present to Blythe.

At Christmas, Kate's brother, Kevin, with his wife, Lindy, and children, Cody and Melissa, came for several days. Mom's brief break in treatments allowed her to feel a little more energetic. No one else was sick, so the family gathered as usual in Mountain View.

Eight-year-old Cody greeted her. "We missed you, Aunt Kate. Why did you stay away so long?" It pleased her that he still allowed her to hug him.

Kate wasn't sure how to explain to her nephew about her attempt to escape the pain of losing Tim and about her new life in Millvale. "I decided to stay in Millvale last Christmas, but that doesn't mean I didn't miss you. You've grown so big!"

He nodded. "Pretty soon I'm going to be taller than Mom." He looked at his mother and straightened to his full height.

"So I see." Kate smiled at her sister-in-law. As she greeted Lindy, she murmured, "It will probably be a few years before that happens."

Melissa tugged on Kate's sleeve. Kate looked down at her. "What about me? Am I getting big?"

Kate picked her up and twirled her around. "Yes, and I see

you're missing some teeth. You must have had a visit from the Tooth Fairy recently." She set her niece down.

"At the rate she's losing teeth, she's going to break the tooth bank pretty soon," Kevin said. "It's good to see you, Sis. You were gone too long."

Kate pulled him in for a hug. "Well, I'm here now."

"I hope you have something to eat, Mom. I'm starved!" Kevin rubbed his stomach.

"You know I'm always prepared for you," his mother replied. "Although Kate did most of the work."

Kevin raised his eyebrows and looked at his sister. "And it's edible? I remember your food experiments when we were kids."

She put her fists on her hips. "Okay, Bro'. I'll have you know I've learned a lot about cooking, and I do a pretty good job too!" She lifted her chin. "Besides, who can mess up soup and sandwiches?"

"That's good!" He laughed.

"I think we'd better plan on an early night. The grandkids will have us up before dawn tomorrow." Kate's father put an arm round each of them.

Lindy turned to her mother-in-law. "The kids know you haven't been feeling well, Mom. They decided to stay in bed in the morning until they are told they can get up. Their idea."

Tears shimmered in her mother's eyes. "My grandchildren are so thoughtful. I'm feeling a little better right now, but sometimes getting up early is hard. Thank you, Cody and Melissa." She held out her arms, and her grandchildren went to her for a hug.

Kate didn't realize until then how much she had missed her family. Seeing her mother so animated while they celebrated Christmas together filled her with a contentment she hadn't experienced for a while. She knew more hard times lay ahead when her mother's treatments started up again.

ON THE DAY AFTER CHRISTMAS, Kate invited her niece and nephew into her studio. They had a painting lesson. Cody was hard at work at his easel, tongue between his teeth. He was trying to paint a picture of his favorite baseball player. Melissa asked to look at Kate's sketch book. "I will be very careful," she promised.

"What do you think, Aunt Kate?" Cody asked, stepping back to give her a view of his work.

Kate smiled. "Pretty good! You have a good eye for perspective, and it looks like your man is ready to hit the ball. You've chosen good colors too."

"What's per . . . per-spec-tive?"

"Some things in your painting look like they're in front, and some look like they're in back, the way they would look if you were there." Kate went on to briefly describe and demonstrate perspective.

Cody picked up his brush again. "You should be an art teacher, Aunt Kate. You explain things really well."

"Who's this, Aunt Kate?" Melissa asked, pointing to Kate's first sketch of Blythe.

Kate turned toward her niece. "That's Blythe Chambers. She lives in Millvale."

"Her front teeth are missing, like mine." Melissa ran her tongue over the space where her front teeth used to be. She turned several pages to a sketch of Jack. "Who's this?"

Kate hesitated. "That's Blythe's uncle Jack."

"Is he your boyfriend, like Tim?"

Kate's eyes widened in surprise. She opened her mouth to answer then closed it.

"Let me see." Cody set down his brush and crossed to where they sat on the loveseat.

Kate took a deep breath, uncertain how to explain. "Blythe's mother died, so Jack helps take care of Blythe when her daddy goes on business trips. She liked to spend time with both of us." She remembered Jack's touch on her cheek and his kiss. "We're just friends." She turned over a few pages. "This is Ellie and her husband, Ben. I worked for her while I lived in Millvale."

"In her flower shop," Melissa said.

"Yes." Kate turned to another page. "This is Blythe's daddy, Mark."

"He looks like Jack," Cody observed.

"That's because they're brothers. Mark's a little older."

Kate showed them drawings of the meadow and Mill Pond. Melissa liked the ducks.

Cody wanted to know more about Kate's drawing of people playing softball. She then shared her photo album with them. Jack had taken most of the pictures. She preferred drawing and painting.

CHAPTER NINE

"What now?" Kate grumbled, throwing the dish towel over her shoulder. Checking the wall clock, she reached for the insistent phone. Who would be calling this early?

She punched the "talk" key and said, "Hello. Greenways'."

"Hi, Katie, it's Ellie."

"Ellie, hi. It's early. Is something wrong?"

"I tried your cell phone, but it wasn't on. I . . . Katie, Blythe passed away last night."

Kate quickly pulled out a kitchen chair and collapsed into it. "What?"

"Blythe, she's gone!"

A sob clogged Kate's throat. She swallowed hard. A picture of the sweet face with brown eyes and dark hair formed in her mind. She shook her head to clear away the fog.

"What happened?" Kate finally managed to say.

Kate could tell Ellie struggled to control her voice. "Word is that she couldn't fight the pneumonia this time. A bout with the flu this winter left her immune system weak."

"I knew she had been sick, but she told me she was getting

89

better." Blythe's last letter had included a delightful picture and plans for a vacation.

"For a while it seemed that way. I saw her in church for a few weeks. It happened so fast," Ellie explained. "I thought you'd want to know."

"I wondered why I stopped getting letters from her. She didn't answer my emails either." Kate sniffed and wiped at her tears. "Poor Mark. How is he?"

"He's devastated. Jack too. Do you think, will you come for the funeral?"

Kate paused before answering. Her father was on a business trip, and her mother's last chemo treatment had left her very weak.

She took a deep breath and let it out slowly. "I don't know. Dad's away, and Mom's very low just now. Millvale is six hours from here. I'm not sure I can make it."

"The funeral is scheduled for Friday morning." Ellie added, "I'm getting so many orders for flowers, I think I may have to special order more. That little girl touched many hearts."

"Dad doesn't get home until late Friday night. I don't think I should leave her."

Kate picked up the dish cloth and began to scrub the already clean counter top. Her conscience pricked her. She wasn't being completely honest with her friend. True, she had important responsibilities in Mountain View. But something else, as well, held her back from returning to Millvale for her little friend's funeral: Jack.

"Well, if you change your mind, you know you can stay with Ben and me. You're always welcome. By the way, Jack has been in the shop a couple of times. He doesn't say much, just wanders around for a few minutes then leaves. Have you had any contact with him since you left?"

"No, Ellie, I wouldn't know what to say. We didn't part on the best terms."

"I just wondered. He looks like a lost soul. I think he misses you."

Kate debated how she should answer her friend. Ellie didn't know how much Jack's rejection had hurt her. Her parting from him played in her mind. She finally said, "I'm here and not going anywhere for the present." Jack knew where to find her.

"I guess that's true." Ellie paused. "Are you still painting?"

"My painting keeps me sane. You know Dad let me set up a studio in the basement. I have a baby monitor so I can hear if Mom needs me."

"I'm sorry we don't live closer so I can help you. We'll try to visit soon. How is your mother?"

"I told you how much she enjoyed the visit from Kevin's family for Christmas. We all did. But reality set in with this new round of therapy. The doctors are hopeful, but she's so thin and weak. I worry about her."

"How are you holding up?"

"The church has been helpful, sending in meals several times a week. And Mom has a couple of friends who stay with her when I have to go on errands. They're great." Tears surfaced. She struggled to hold them back. "To be honest, Ellie, I'm tired. I'm glad I can help Mom and Dad, but after living independently for a year, it's hard living with them again. But it won't be forever." She sighed. "Why does life have to be so hard?"

"I think the hard times are to test our faith and help us depend more on God." She paused. "Well, I have to open the shop now. I thought you'd want to know about Blythe. We'll all miss her."

"Yes, we will. She was like the meadow full of wildflowers. I wish I could be there. Okay, Ellie. Thank you so much for calling. Thank you for listening to me. I'll let you go. Bye."

Kate punched the "off" key on the phone and sobbed as she leaned on the table. "It hurts, God. I feel broken all over again. Why did you let her die?"

She took a deep breath and stood, wanting to talk to her mother about Blythe. She peeked in the bedroom where her mother slept, her relaxed features masking some of her recent suffering. Sleep was a valuable commodity in this household, so Kate didn't attempt to awaken the invalid. Instead, she headed for her studio.

Kate wandered around the room. Outside the window, the sun peeked from behind snow clouds to shine on the neighbor's house and reflect off piles of snow. On the mountains in the background, bare deciduous trees blended with the dark green of evergreens. She picked up and put down brushes and turned around to look at the finished paintings lined up along the wall, thinking about her year in Millvale. When she spotted her sketch book, she began to flip through it. She stopped at the drawing of Blythe playing among the wildflowers in the meadow.

"I wondered why you had stopped writing," Kate whispered, one finger tracing the outline of the child's face.

Kate had faithfully answered every "letter," and she had kept a folder of Blythe's drawings and paintings. She now opened the folder and withdrew Blythe's last letter, smiling at the childish scrawl. Mark or Jack must have helped her. Blythe's drawings illustrated her words.

Der Kate

I had flu, but I'm betr now.

Thank you for the pichur book you are a good artist can you cum see me me and Daddy will go to the beach we will fly kites and hav fun I wish you culd cum.

Blythe Amber Chambers

Kate gazed tenderly at Blythe's painting of a little girl running down a beach with a kite flying behind her. The tears continued to flow. She rubbed them from her cheeks with her fingers. The run on the beach would never be.

Sorrow washed over her again. Sorrow that Blythe had suffered, that she was gone. Sorrow for the bereft father, all alone now. Sorrow about how her time in Millvale had ended and why she had to return home. After using a tissue to dry her tears, Kate carefully tore the drawing of Blythe picking flowers in the meadow from the sketch book. She placed it in a manila envelope with a note expressing her own sorrow, trying to convey her sympathy for Mark in his time of loss. She addressed the envelope, hoping he would like this picture of his daughter. How do you comfort a father who has lost a child? Especially when this same man had already lost his wife.

And how about Jack? He had loved Blythe so deeply, his heart must be bleeding. She longed to hold him and comfort him. She touched her lips at the memory of his parting kiss.

Kate wiped her eyes as she uncovered her current work, an acrylic of Blythe feeding the ducks on Mill Pond. Blythe had loved to watch the ducks. A fresh wave of sorrow washed over her. She replaced the cover on the canvas.

Curling into the corner of the old, green love seat in her studio, she thought of Blythe listening to the wind singing through the blue spruce in the meadow. A painting of this hung in her room. She remembered the day Blythe had become a part of her life, the day Kate first painted the meadow.

Kate pulled another tissue from the box. She had been able to set aside the hurt of Jack's rejection, for the most part, until now. Her relationship with Blythe and Blythe's uncle had been closely tied. Ellie's call about Blythe's death had reopened the wound. She didn't know if Jack thought about her or missed her. Oh, why wouldn't he take a chance on love?

No sound came from her mother through the monitor, but Kate climbed the stairs to check on her. She paused for a moment to look at the mountains through the living room window. "I will lift up my eyes to the hills—from whence comes my help? My help comes from the Lord," she said softly to herself. A light snowfall had refreshed the landscape.

Finding her mother still quietly asleep, Kate pulled a bottle of water from the refrigerator and an apple from the fruit bowl on the table. Back in her studio, she leafed through her sketchpad, stopping at a drawing of Jack blowing bubbles with Blythe. This was the Jack she loved. Affectionate, fun-loving, caring. Kate remembered the summer day when she had drawn this picture. They went to the meadow for a picnic, and Jack had brought along a bottle of bubble soap for each of them. The soft breeze whispered through the trees, and fluffy white clouds floated across the blue sky to the accompaniment of giggles from the little girl at play.

They had been so close that day, and Kate knew Jack loved her, even though he never said the words. She could see it in his eyes when he looked at her, in his voice when he spoke to her, and in his touch when he held her hand. Her heart sang in harmony with the wind in the blue spruce. That day she had hope, but it seemed he had not loved her enough nor trusted God enough to overcome his fear of loving and losing. She had returned to Mountain View, rejected and alone. Afraid to go back.

AFTER ELLIE'S PHONE CALL, Kate mourned for Blythe. Her canvas remained covered, her paints and brushes untouched. On several mornings when she awoke, she found her pillow damp with tears. She busied herself with cleaning and organizing the house until her mother, sitting propped up by pillows on her bed, called to her.

"Kate, come sit down for a while." She patted the bed, inviting her daughter to sit beside her.

"I'm sorry, Kate. I know you want to be there for her funeral. I'm sorry to be such a problem." It was Friday, and her mother knew Kate's heart was in Millvale.

"Please don't say that, Mom. I'm glad to be able to help you." She reached over to take her mother's thin and fragile outstretched hand. "It's just that Blythe was special. I hoped that one day you could meet her. But now . . ." Fresh tears flowed, and Kate pulled a tissue from her pocket.

"I feel like I know her, you have told me so much about her. I will meet her one day."

Her mother held Kate's warm hand between her own cool hands.

Kate nodded. "I know. I wish I had gone back to see her before this." She paused. "You know, I think what I missed most in the year I spent in Millvale was our talks."

"I missed you too. You had us worried. You shut yourself away, and then you left. I know you felt you had to go away, but I'm glad you're back."

Kate sat on the bed next to her mother, her head resting against the pillow. She laid her arm across her mother, and they sat quietly together for a few minutes.

"I miss my little girl, but I'm so proud of the woman you've become. I love you, Kate."

"I love you, too, Mom."

Kate closed her eyes and tried to picture the service in Millvale.

MILLVALE COMMUNITY CHURCH FILLED QUICKLY. Jack watched his brother greet fellow mourners as they entered. Mark, a man anguished by his own loss, offered comfort to the friends who honored the memory of his daughter. By offering comfort to others, he seemed to find strength for himself. Jack knew his brother demonstrated a scriptural principle, that God offers believers comfort so they are able to offer comfort to one another in times of trouble. But Jack had seen the suffering in his brother's eyes. Nearly numb with grief himself, he wondered how his brother would make it through the memorial service for Blythe. He worried that Mark would give up on life without the presence of his little girl. Although he carried his own grief, Jack knew he had to be strong for Mark.

Would Kate come? More than anyone else, he longed for her. He needed her smile, her touch, her comfort. She had loved Blythe too. Mark displayed Kate's drawing of the girl in a frame on top of the closed casket. Surely Kate would come to say goodbye. He glanced repeatedly toward the door and tried to dismiss the thought that he should have called her.

Ellie and Ben arrived with a few last bouquets. After they had placed the flowers, Jack approached them.

"Jack." Ellie embraced their friend. "How are you?"

Ben's hand rested on Jack's shoulder. "We're with you, brother."

Jack opened his mouth to ask about Kate. Before he could speak, Ellie said, "I talked to Kate. She won't be able to come." Ellie must have read disappointment on his face, because she explained, "Her mother has been going through a difficult time, and her father won't be home until late tonight. She didn't feel she could come all this way and leave her mother."

Jack's shoulders slumped. He nodded. "I see. I hoped, I thought she might come." If only he had followed through on his idea to visit Mountain View with his niece. Getting his business started had taken priority. Now it was too late for Blythe, and maybe for him.

"Believe me, she would be here if she could," Ellie assured him.

"Jack!" Mark called to him.

Ellie and Ben found seats, and Jack joined his brother. The

two of them walked to the front of the church and sat together. Pastor Clary approached the pulpit and began the service.

All the words of comfort couldn't fill the empty place in Jack's heart reserved just for Kate.

~

ELLIE CALLED Kate that evening to tell her about the memorial service.

"It was so beautiful, but so sad. Blythe touched the lives of so many people. I don't think there was a dry eye. Even Pastor Clary had to stop for a minute. I remembered the verse in the Bible that talks about God collecting tears in His bottle. I think His bottle overflowed this afternoon. We all needed His comfort. Oh, and Mark put up that picture of Blythe you sent."

"He did? I hoped he would like it." Through the living room picture window, Kate noticed the moonlit patches of snow on the mountains, up to the tree line.

"He did. We all did. You captured Blythe's spirit. I thought Blythe might walk out of the picture and start talking to us."

"I'm glad it helped." Kate swallowed and wiped her tears. She heard Ellie sniff.

"How is your mother?"

"Today was a good day. She'll finish chemo soon and have a few radiation treatments."

"When she's feeling well enough, we'll come for a visit," Ellie promised.

Kate felt better after talking with Ellie. They discussed everybody and everything, except Jack.

During the weeks that followed, she wondered if she had any chance with Jack now.

~

"WHAT'S THIS?" Mark picked up the paper Jack had just tossed into his lap. He glanced at it and then at his brother.

"Just something for you to consider. I've been on the Internet. There's a bereavement support group over in Wellsburg. I think you need to go." Jack waited in front of his brother's chair.

Mark read the information. "No, Jack, I don't think so."

"Look, Mark, I know you're hurting. All you do is sit around here, at least most of the time. I'm worried about you."

Mark gazed at the photograph of his wife, daughter, and himself taken shortly before Rachael's death. Jack thought his brother had forgotten his presence when Mark said, "I don't think you understand how I feel."

That hurt. Jack knew he had loved both Rachael and Blythe. Sure, he was only the brother-in-law and uncle, but his heart still bled. Jack also knew it wasn't the time to defend himself. He intended to see that his brother got the help he needed to work through his grief. It felt strange to Jack to be taking the role of advisor when it had always been Mark, the older brother, who had handed out the advice.

"No, I guess I can't understand completely, but you know I miss them too. I think you spend more time wanting to be with them than living. But your life is still here, Mark, and being able to talk to other grieving people or a counselor will help you."

Jack waited for a response. Mark refused to look at him. Jack continued. "Look, I think it would help both of us. Why don't we try it together, at least once or twice? If it doesn't help, we don't have to go again."

This time Mark shifted in his seat and finally he looked at Jack. "All right. I'll try it. I don't think it will help, but I know you mean well." Mark's mouth turned up in a grin, the first Jack had seen in quite a while. "Thanks for looking after me, Little Brother. I guess I haven't been very good company lately."

"You've got that right. I'd like my brother back. Life is pretty lonely without him."

"One thing I do know, Jack. Although my heart aches, I do not regret having loved Rachael and Blythe. I miss them so much." He stopped momentarily, biting his lip and taking a deep breath. "But they are here, in my heart." He laid his hand over his heart. "I have memories. They made my life so full and added purpose and meaning. I hope you will experience that too."

Jack stood and walked around the room, his hands in his pockets. "I've been thinking a lot about Kate lately. I've tried to forget her, Mark, and I've tried to pretend she's just a friend. Maybe I did make a mistake." He shrugged. "Maybe it's too late for us. Maybe she's found someone else by now."

"So, what's your plan?"

"I don't have one yet. But I think I'll get my business going, then I'll pay a visit to Mountain View."

"It's good not to rush into a relationship or marriage, but don't wait too long, Jack. And if you need a shove, I'm here. I'm sure there are a few others who would join me."

Jack smiled at the thought of Mrs. Matthews and Ellie cheering him on and of Blythe in heaven clapping her support.

CHAPTER TEN

As spring approached and her mother's health improved, Kate and her father sat in the living room one evening. Mom was in bed. She still needed a lot of sleep.

"Kate, what are your plans after this?" he asked, laying down the magazine he'd been reading.

Kate closed her book. She ran her hand over the cover. "I'm not sure, Dad." Shaking her head, she added, "I'm not planning to go back to Millvale."

"Didn't Ellie say she would hold the job for you?"

Kate nodded. "Yes." She stood up and walked over to look out the picture window. She had always loved this view of the mountains. They reminded her of God's majesty and strength, and their beauty touched her artist's heart.

"Broken hearts are hard to mend, right?" he said gently.

Kate looked over her shoulder at her father. "How did you know? I didn't say anything."

"When you lost Tim, it was like a light went out. You had lost the one you loved and your hope for the future. I know when you left to go to Millvale, you couldn't bear to be reminded every moment about what you had lost. When you talk about the little girl, Blythe, there is a special light in your eyes whenever you mention her uncle Jack. You're hesitant to go back, even though you liked working for Ellie. What happened, Katie?"

"I didn't realize I revealed that much." Kate's eyes returned to the mountains. "When I moved to Millvale, I pretty much stayed by myself, except when I worked for Ellie and went to church with her."

"You had to work through the grief process."

"Yes." She turned to face her father. "Yes. It took almost a year before I started painting again. Ellie sent me to a beautiful spot, a meadow surrounded by blue spruce trees on a dirt road outside Millvale. That's where Blythe found me."

Her dad chuckled. "She found you?"

"Yes. It sounds funny to say it that way. She lived in a cottage up the road, and when she saw me painting, she had to come to see what I was doing. Her mother had done some painting, so I think that's what drew her. Of course, she shouldn't have left her yard. Jack came looking for her. Blythe's mother had died, and Jack helped take care of Blythe when Mark was away."

Kate hesitated, waiting for her father's response. He patted the sofa beside him, and she sat down.

"Blythe made me want to live again. She was so excited about life. I realized then that I wasn't the only one to have lost a loved one. After that, my anger at God disappeared. Blythe always wanted the three of us to spend time together." Kate smiled as memories surfaced. "She was very persuasive in a sweet and loving way. We spent a lot of time together."

Kate paused, picturing the handsome face with blue eyes. "Jack is fun-loving, considerate, and caring. You'd like him, Dad. I tried to be careful, always feeling he had put up some sort of barrier, but I fell in love again." A lump formed in Kate's throat. "Jack's afraid to love me, Dad. He's lost several important people in his life. He's afraid that God will take away someone else he loves. It's hard to lose someone you love." Tears filled her eyes. "But I know it would be harder not to love at all."

"You probably understand how he feels. But you don't feel the same way, and that hurts."

Kate nodded. "I left angry and disappointed. I'm not totally without hope that Jack will change his mind, but . . ."

Her father sighed. "It's hard to wait, isn't it? Sometimes God's timing seems so long."

She snuggled against him. "Thanks for understanding and caring, Dad. How did you get to be so wise?"

He put his arm around her shoulders and squeezed. "God's Word and life's experiences are good teachers, although I think I still have a lot to learn." He turned to hold Kate by the shoulders so he could look into her eyes. "I'm glad you're able to love again after losing Tim. I think he'd want you to go on with your life."

Kate dried her eyes with a tissue. She chuckled as she handed the box to her father.

As he pulled a tissue from the box and wiped his eyes, he said, "Being emotional comes with age, I guess." He patted her knee. "Now, why don't you take some of your paintings down to the gift shop tomorrow? Jonathan Weeks might be willing to display some of them for you. I spoke with him the other day. He said he wants to encourage local talent."

"You talked to Jonathan about my paintings?" She leaned forward. "Do you think I should? I'm not sure anyone would buy them."

"Nonsense! Besides, you won't know until you try. I'd like to see you do something for yourself. You've given so much to your mother and me in the last six months. Don't be afraid to take a step of faith into the future."

Kate said goodnight, her heart filled with thankfulness for her parents. Even though she still lived with them, they treated her as an adult. They understood why she had left Mountain View after Tim's death. It touched her deeply that her father took the time to think about her as he dealt with his own trials.

❧

KATE NEARLY HUGGED Jonathan Weeks when he agreed to display some of her paintings for possible sale. They had known each other for many years, although Jonathan was a little older.

"You've really developed your painting. Local residents and tourists will buy these, I'm sure." He held up one of the three paintings she had brought to show him. "The Chamber of Commerce wants to build tourism in the area."

She chose six of her best work, three of the local area and three of Millvale, framed them, and took them to the gift shop.

To her surprise and delight, people began looking for and buying her paintings. She didn't get rich from the sales, but she appreciated the return on her efforts. The local newspaper featured a story about her work.

"The Four Seasons Gallery in Oakwood is interested in your paintings," Jonathan told her the next day when she stopped by. "Mr. Lake came in yesterday. He read the newspaper feature story on you, and he said he is interested in doing a show of regional artists and artisans. I showed him your paintings. He would like to meet with you and see a portfolio."

Kate's eyes widened. "Wow! Really? The Four Seasons Gallery opened when I was in high school. As a student, I dreamed about having my own show there. I would sit on a bench and pretend my paintings hung on the walls. A couple of them did during student shows."

The gift shop proprietor handed her a business card. "Here's his card. You call him and make an appointment and do it soon."

She stared at the card. "Thank you, Jonathan." As she left the shop, she felt as though she were floating on air, unsure whether she'd ever stop smiling.

~

AFTER CHEMOTHERAPY ENDED, followed by a few radiation treatments, her mother's appetite and energy levels increased. As her mother's health continued to improve, Kate invited Ellie and Ben to visit. They came in March.

"I'm so glad you could come," Kate greeted her friends. "I've missed you. Mom is looking forward to your visit."

"We decided to make this trip like the second part of our honeymoon." Ben put his arm around Ellie and pulled her close. "We're going to do some sight-seeing on the way back, and we'll stop at a flower show."

"Business is slow, so I closed for the week. The mad rush will start soon, with spring coming. My customers had plenty of notice, so I'm not worried," Ellie said.

While her mother napped, Kate sent her father out to get some ice cream for dinner. Ben joined him, so Kate and Ellie had time alone to talk. She could say things to Ellie she wouldn't say to anyone else.

"I'm excited, Ellie. Jonathan Weeks took some of my paintings for his gift shop, and I might have a gallery show this summer. And look at this newspaper story." She handed her friend a copy of the article as they sat in her studio.

"Do you think you'll be coming back to Millvale?" Ellie read the story and handed the clipping back to her. "I still have an opening for you if you want it."

"No, Ellie, I plan to stay in Mountain View for now. I'm getting more opportunities for my painting. You might as well hire someone else." She hugged her friend. "I want you to know I appreciate all you've done for me."

"I thought that might be your answer, but I wanted to know

for sure. I miss you. Mrs. Matthews has asked about you several times. Everyone misses you, even Jack. Did you know he's starting his own business, JC Computers?"

"Blythe had mentioned it in one of her letters. I'm not surprised. He told me that was his goal." She didn't comment on Jack missing her. She missed him terribly, but she feared another rejection. He needed to take the first step in renewing their relationship, if and when he was ready. If she had gone to the funeral, maybe she could have pushed him along a bit.

The sunshine and cool air held the promise of spring as Kate escorted Ellie and Ben around Mountain View. On their drive to the Four Seasons Gallery in Oakwood, they passed a white cross marker.

"This is where Tim died." The spot still evoked sadness within Kate. "I don't know who put it up."

Ellie looked over her shoulder. "Are you all right?"

"I'm okay. I have good memories of Tim. I feel sad sometimes, but it doesn't hurt like it used to."

The couple caught Kate up on the news from Millvale. They shared what little information they had about Alana, who was at that time located in a remote area with little outside contact. And, happily, her mother felt well enough to be able to enjoy their visit.

Their time together flew by. "God has been so good to us," Kate said as she hugged her friends goodbye. "Thank you for your visit. I feel refreshed, like I've taken a breath of crisp air." Ellie promised to try to be there for Kate's gallery show when it was scheduled.

KATE WALKED to the cemetery to lay a red and a white rose on Tim's grave. Where would she be and what would she be doing right now if she had married Tim? Sweet memories brought a smile to her lips. Later in the day she visited Tim's parents and gave them a portrait she had painted of him.

The next day Kate awoke to the patter of rain against her window. She decided the time had come to face the past. Going to the attic, she lugged down eight plastic totes that had been stored there since her departure for Millvale. Taking a deep breath, she opened the first and plunged in. Laughing at some of the things she found, she sorted through her treasures, old school papers, awards and certificates from her life before Tim, discarding three-quarters of them. She saved most of her art work.

"What's all this?" Her mother asked when she came down the stairs carrying four full garbage bags.

Kate laughed. "The garbage men will wonder too. I decided it was time to clean out, and today was a good day for it. Here is the evidence of hard work." She set down the bags. "I separated recyclables, and there's more." She sneezed and coughed. "I stirred up some dust, I guess." She grabbed a tissue from the box on the coffee table.

Her mother's eyebrows rose. "More?"

Kate nodded, knowing the hardest was yet to come.

As she sorted through her memories with Tim, she stopped frequently to wipe her eyes and blow her nose. She ran her fingers over the vase and bowl Tim had fashioned for her on the potter's wheel. Perhaps one day she would display them in her home. She carefully put together a scrapbook of pictures, cards, event tickets, and even a wedding invitation. She tenderly packed away her memorials, along with her bridal gown enclosed in a garment bag, fitting them all into one container.

Kate gazed at the lacy bodice of the gown. Should she try to sell it? She would never wear it, and it seemed a shame to waste it by leaving it packed away. As she looked around to see if she had everything, Kate noticed her engagement portrait with Tim on her dresser. She picked up the framed photograph, rubbing her fingers over the smooth wood of the frame and then across the glass covering the photo. "I loved you so much, Tim," she whispered, lying down with the picture in her hands. "We really felt this way, so full of love and joy. We had so many dreams for the future." Kate didn't know how long she lay there, hugging the photo, remembering. She sighed. "It just wasn't to be." With her fingertips she transferred a kiss from her lips to the photo. She got up and laid the picture face down on top of the white gown wrapped in the garment bag. She snapped the lid of the large, blue tote closed.

By dinnertime, when her father returned from work, five empty and three full plastic totes had been returned to the attic. Six full garbage bags stood in the garage. Kate felt she had said her final goodbye to the past.

A few days later, Kate stopped to see Tim's mother. Emily Barrows greeted her with a smile and invited her in. As they entered the living room, Kate spoke. "I've been cleaning out, Mrs. Barrows. I thought you and Mr. Barrows would like to have these pictures of Tim." She handed an envelope to Tim's mother.

The older woman seated herself and hugged the envelope to her before drawing out the photos to look at them. "Thank you so much, Kate. We'll add them to our memory scrapbook."

She set them aside. "How are you, dear?" She patted the sofa next to her, and Kate joined her.

Even as a child, Kate had admired Emily Barrows. The older woman, a former school teacher, appeared delicate. Kate knew her as a gracious woman of faith, stamina, and capability. Emily's graying hair framed her face with soft waves, and the pale pink tunic she wore with blue jeans added a glow to her complexion.

"I'm fine," Kate said.

"How is your mother?"

Kate smiled. "She's doing quite well. Her treatments are finished, so she's beginning to feel better. She has put on a few pounds and has a lot more energy, although she has to be careful not to overdo. She has started going to church again. And her hair is growing back. She has an appointment to see the hair-dresser later this week."

"I'm glad to hear that. I haven't been able to speak to her at church. I know she's had a rough time. She must be happy to have you back home."

"Yes, I think so. My mom was always there for me, I'm glad I could help. Why don't you come and visit her sometime?"

"Yes, I will." The older woman folded her hands. When she looked up at Kate, she had tears in her eyes. "I'm sorry you couldn't become my daughter-in-law. Please, don't be a stranger here. I'd love to have you visit."

Kate bit her lip. "I'd like that too." Her voice quavered.

Tim's mother looked down at her hands then up at her. "Kate, I'm sure Tim would want you to be happy. Tim's gone, but you're alive. If you find love again, don't reject it for Tim's sake."

Kate leaned over and hugged her. If only she knew. There had been no promises between her and Jack. She did not feel she had the right to speak about him.

Emily touched Kate's arm. "Do you think, could you . . .? Jenny adored her big brother. You know that." Kate nodded. "I think Jenny has had the hardest time accepting her brother's death. She seems still angry, even bitter at times." Emily paused and shook her head. "We've talked to her, and she went to the pastor for counseling."

Kate had seen Jenny only in church since returning to Mountain View. She remembered the fun they used to have together, even with their age difference, before Tim's death. Jenny could hardly wait to be a bridesmaid and wear her gown in the wedding. Nine years younger than her brother, Jenny considered Tim her hero. Kate hadn't thought much about Jenny in the past two years. How could she have been so selfish, so inconsiderate of the girl, only thirteen when her beloved brother had died?

Emily continued, "I wondered if you would talk to Jenny, take her out for ice cream or something. Maybe you can help her. She used to look up to you. Will you try?"

Kate knew about her own parents' concern for her, so she could understand better how Jenny's mother felt. "Of course I will. I should have taken time with Jenny before now, even before I went to Millvale. I'm sorry. I've been so wrapped up in myself, I didn't even try to help her." She hadn't meant to be so thoughtless and selfish. She needed to talk to Jenny as soon as possible.

"We've all needed time to grieve, but Jenny's young and has her life ahead of her. She has to get past this in order to go on." Emily smiled at her. "Thank you for coming today."

Kate, at twenty-four, felt old when she noticed that the majority of the single young adults she knew in Mountain View were younger than she. Most of her former friends and class-mates had married or moved away. With her painting career her focus and Jack on her heart, dating lay low on her list of priori-ties. Without conscious effort, she became "big sister" to the young men and women in the singles' ministry at church. Now she hoped God might use her to help Jenny.

Kate didn't try to draw attention to herself. She liked to help people, but she usually worked behind the scenes. She prayed for wisdom. Confronting Jenny would mean stepping out of her comfort zone, and it could leave her vulnerable to rejection once again.

CHAPTER ELEVEN

On the Sunday following her visit with Emily Barrows, Kate left the church building with her parents. She saw Jenny come out of the building, talking and laughing with a group of teens.

"I'll be home in a little while. I have to talk with Jenny Barrows."

"Okay," Dad said. "We'll see you at home then." Her parents walked on, arm-in-arm.

As she observed Jenny with her friends, Kate wondered if Mrs. Barrows had been imagining Jenny's lingering anger. The girl smiled, reminding Kate of Tim. Jenny looked up. The smile faded into a frown as she watched Kate approach her.

Kate took a deep breath and smiled. "Hello, Jenny."

Jenny glanced at her friends. "Hi," she said sullenly and turned her back on Kate.

Before the teen could get away, Kate stepped toward her and touched her shoulder. "Jenny, can we talk?"

Reluctantly, Jenny said goodbye to her friends, crossed her arms, and waited. Jenny's brown hair, as well as her hazel eyes and smile, reminded Kate so much of Tim. Jenny had left behind the awkwardness of thirteen to become an attractive fifteen, with a slender figure and shining, carefully arranged hair. Kate realized she wouldn't be dealing with a little girl.

"How have you been, Jenny?"

Jenny shrugged. "What do you care?"

The girl's words hit Kate like a punch in the gut. "I'm sorry, Jenny. I know I haven't acted as though I care, but I really do."

Jenny shrugged again. "So?"

This is going well. Help, Lord! "I wondered if we can get together sometime. Maybe go for ice cream. You do still like ice cream?" Kate remembered that the girl had never refused ice cream two years ago. She thought Jenny might refuse now.

Jenny wouldn't make eye contact. "I don't know. I'm really busy." She turned away. Kate's heart sank. "I know, Jenny, but I'd like to talk."

The girl looked over her shoulder. "About what?"

"What has happened in the past two years. About Tim."

"My brother is dead! What good will it do to talk about him?" Jenny started to walk away. Kate placed her hand on the girl's arm to stop her. "What?" Jenny whirled back with a frown.

Kate took a deep breath. "Jenny, please. I think we have a lot to talk about. Just give me a chance, okay?" Kate looked away and blinked as tears filled her eyes.

The tears seemed to soften Jenny. The girl looked down. "Okay. When?"

"How about tomorrow after school, or maybe next Saturday afternoon?"

Jenny thought a moment before saying, "I have track practice after school tomorrow, but I think Saturday's good."

"You're on the track team?" Jenny nodded at Kate's question. "May I come to a track meet?" Finally, an opening to reach the girl.

"You really want to come to a track meet?"

"Of course. When?"

"This week is our first meet here in Mountain View. It's at four on Tuesday. I'm a runner. I'm working hard to improve my time, but I also like the pole vault. Tim was good at that." A smile lit Jenny's face, and her eyes danced. "You remembered how much I like ice cream."

Kate raised her eyebrows. "Pole vault?" At the girl's nod, she said. "I'm proud of you. Let's plan to go for ice cream on Saturday about one." She had hoped to meet with Jenny sooner. The five days between today and Saturday gave a lot of time for Jenny to find an excuse to change her mind.

"Okay." Jenny started to walk away. She turned back. "Thanks, Kate. I'm really glad you came back."

Kate couldn't resist putting her arm around the girl's shoulders. "Me too, Jenny."

To Kate's surprise, Jenny didn't pull back. Instead she returned the hug.

After the evening worship service, Kate joined a group of young adults at the local pizza shop. Amid all the joking, teasing and chatter, Kate suddenly realized how much she had missed being with friends. Not at all sorry that she had come back to care for her mother, Kate savored her new freedom to go out with other young adults.

"Are you enjoying yourself?" A deep voice spoke from beside her as she waited for the pizza to be served.

Startled, she turned her head to look into twinkling, gray eyes. "Yes." Kate couldn't resist smiling back at him. Until he spoke, she hadn't noticed the young man seated beside her. A discussion with a couple across the table from her had held her attention.

"I'm Wayne Quinn."

"Kate Greenway."

"I know. I'm glad to finally meet you. I've seen you in church."

"Are you new here?" She'd been too busy to keep track of new young men in town.

"Moved here about a month ago. I manage a bookstore over in Oakwood. I understand you're an artist, and you've been taking care of your mother."

Somewhat flattered that he had been interested enough to find out about her, his knowledge of her when she had just met him unnerved her a bit. Rescued by the arrival of the pizzas, she took part in the general chatter as she ate. She soon became comfortable talking with Wayne, steering away from personal to more general topics.

"The next time you're in Oakwood, you should stop in. The bookstore has a fine selection of books on painting. If we don't have a book in stock, we can probably order it," he said.

"I might do that. I like to browse even if I don't buy. Where are you located?"

"Right on Main Street. You can't miss our sign."

"So, how did you become a bookstore manager?" She took a bite of pizza.

"I've always loved books. I have a degree in library science, but I wanted to try the retail angle of books, at least for a while. When I found this position open, it seemed like a God-send."

They became involved in a discussion with others in their group about next month's bowling party and other planned activities.

As they stood to leave, Wayne offered to take her home.

"Thanks for the offer, but no, I have my car, and I have to take several people home." She removed her car keys from her purse.

"Maybe another time, then," he said.

～

ALTHOUGH HER MOTHER'S health improved each day, Kate still had the major responsibility for cooking and housework. She took the time to paint a portrait of Tim in watercolors, a gift for Jenny, to give her on Saturday. As she painted, she realized how much her skill had developed over the past year. She preferred using acrylics, but she occasionally used oils or watercolors. Kate also spent a lot of time putting together a portfolio to show Mr. Lake when she went for her appointment to discuss the gallery show.

Mid-week she awoke to the sound of her mother coughing. The doctor assured them it was an upper respiratory infection and gave her a prescription for medication to help relieve the symptoms. Only somewhat reassured, Kate watched her mother carefully, cringing when coughs shook the woman's frail body and worrying about fever. By the time her father returned home on Friday night, her mother seemed a little better, and Kate was ready for a day off.

Kate breathed deeply of the perfumed, sun-kissed, spring air as she left the house just before one o'clock on Saturday afternoon. The mild, late-April weather was coaxing trees into leaf and flowers into bloom. The mountain forests displayed tints of green and red. Shouts of childish laughter reached her ears, and she smiled to think that Blythe would be begging to go to the meadow on a day like today. Two tears tracked down her cheeks. She wiped her face with her hand and shook her head to make Jack's image disappear from her mind.

Jenny waited at a small table outside the ice cream shop. One of her friends stopped and spoke to her. Jenny pointed to Kate, and the other girl turned to look at her. Kate recognized her as a teen from church and waved to her. The girl waved back, spoke to Jenny again, and walked on.

A smile lit Jenny's face. "Hi," she said.

"Hi, yourself. Are you ready for some ice cream?"

Jenny giggled and stood. "You bet! There's always room for ice cream."

A few minutes later, they exited the shop and walked to the small park, licking their cones. The rose bushes had not yet bloomed, the leaves still small. Kate knew the mother duck, within the protective parameters of a white picket fence, would be hatching her brood of ducklings soon. Ducks always made their way to water, even to small ponds in small towns. Again, Kate thought of Blythe, and as they sat down on the park bench under a sugar maple with tiny leaves, she had to fight back tears. Childish laughter came from a game of tag behind them.

"Are you okay, Kate?" Concern edged Jenny's voice.

Kate waited for the tears to recede. "When I lived in Millvale, I knew a little girl named Blythe. On a day like today she would want to play in the meadow, and she loved to watch the ducks on the mill pond in town." The ducks also reminded her of Jack, but she didn't say so.

"Maybe she's playing in the meadow today."

"No, not today." Kate shook her head and sighed. "Blythe died a few weeks ago."

"That's sad." Jenny licked her cone to catch the drips of bubble gum ice cream.

"Yes, she was only seven. She was so full of life and love." Kate took a lick of her berry swirl, rescuing her blouse from a drip. "I like to think of her playing and singing in a meadow of wildflowers in heaven." She smiled as the happy picture formed in her mind.

Jenny paused a moment then said thoughtfully, "Why do you think God let her die?"

Kate realized she had her opening. She pulled her photo album from her quilted patchwork bag. "May I show you some pictures of Blythe?"

"Sure." Jenny slid closer to Kate on the park bench.

Kate finished her ice cream and carefully wiped her fingers so she wouldn't soil the precious pictures.

"Blythe's mother had died, so she lived with her father, Mark, in a storybook cottage near a lovely meadow. Blythe played there, we had picnics, picked strawberries, blew bubbles. I painted there a lot." As Kate told her story, she imagined herself at the meadow. She closed her eyes and heard Blythe's laughter and the trees' song. She paused.

"This is the place in some of your paintings in the gift shop. She's the little girl in several of the pictures." Jenny touched Blythe's smiling face with her fingertip. "She looks so happy."

"Wildflowers pattern the grass in the meadow, and Blythe always said the blue spruce trees around the meadow sing." Kate looked at her companion. "To be honest, Jenny, Blythe helped me to start living after Tim died. She helped me to have joy and love again. God put her in my life, I think, to make me see that I could move forward with my life." She didn't mention Jack.

Jenny blurted out, "So you just forgot about my brother?" The teen turned her head away.

Kate heard the anger in her voice. "Jenny, I'll never forget Tim. I loved him and planned to marry him." She laid her hand gently on the girl's arm. "I've learned that grief is a process. We have to get through the anger and blame so we can go forward with living."

Jenny covered her face with her hands and sobbed. "I still don't understand why he had to die. I hate that drunk driver. I'm glad he's in prison. He deserved it."

"Oh, Jenny." Kate pulled the grieving girl into her arms. "You're right, he deserved to be punished because he broke the law by being drunk and driving. His sin killed someone we loved."

Jenny accepted the embrace. When she pulled back, Kate handed her a tissue from her bag.

"God has taught me so much in the last two years. I was

angry with God and with the drunk driver. It was unfair that Tim died. We had so many plans for the future, and everything came crashing down that night. I left Mountain View because I felt like I would suffocate here. I ran away from the pain, but it followed me to Millvale." Kate swallowed the lump forming in her throat.

Jenny watched her with narrowed eyes. "You left, and I thought you were mad at me." She shrugged off Kate's hand. "You never talked to me or came to see me. I thought you hated me. I had to stay here alone."

Guilt jolted her. She remembered Jenny's stricken face at the funeral. In her own grief, by refusing to share her grief with Tim's little sister, she had made Jenny feel rejected. If only she had taken time for a few kind words or even an extra hug. If only. Kate shook her head.

"I'm sorry. I didn't think about anyone else, just myself," she confessed. "I'm sorry I hurt you. Will you forgive me?"

The girl brushed her lips with a lock of hair. After a moment she nodded. "Yes."

Kate let out her breath. "Thank you, Jenny. That means so much. You need to let go of your anger and the hate as well. It may not matter to the man in prison, but it will take root in your heart and ruin your life."

Kate paused, asking God for the right words. "You and I do wrong things, too, like the drunk driver. Oh, I don't mean we drink and drive and kill someone. But we're selfish, speak thoughtlessly, want our own way, get angry. We don't deserve forgiveness, but God forgives us. That's why Jesus Christ died on the cross and rose again. If He forgives you and me for so much, don't you think you could forgive the man who killed Tim?"

Jenny shrugged. "I've known that in my head, but my heart still wants to hate. Mom and Dad told me I had to let it go. I even talked to Pastor Michaels." The girl stood, took a few steps, and turned. "Will you help me, Kate? Most of the time I can cover up my real feelings. My friends don't know how I really feel. I miss my brother so much. It's not fair!" Jenny thumped her fist against the back of the park bench.

Kate understood Jenny's anger. She took Jenny's hand and drew her down again. "Life isn't fair. Bad things happen. But God's plan is to give us a full and meaningful life. Anger and bitterness keep us from what God has planned. I think that's what I had to learn when I lived in Millvale. With God's touch, the pain of loss lessens with time, even though the memories remain. Blythe loved her mother and missed her, but it didn't hold her back from enjoying life."

The two friends sat quietly together. Then Kate said, "On my way here, I wondered if Blythe has met Tim yet, in Heaven."

"Maybe." Jenny paused then added, "I never really thought seriously about Heaven, even after Tim died. I just knew he wasn't here. He's there, isn't he, with Jesus?" Kate nodded. "So maybe Blythe and Tim are having fun in Heaven together?" Jenny smiled.

"Yes. Maybe. And if you have received Jesus as your Savior, you'll go to Heaven one day and see Tim again."

"I knew that, at least I had been told that, but I haven't thought much about it before." The girl laid her hand over her heart. "Now I know, in here, that it's true."

Kate squeezed Jenny's shoulder. "I didn't think much about dying when I was your age either." She lifted her quilted bag. "Jenny, I have something for you, if you want it."

"What is it?" The teen watched as, from her bag, Kate pulled a package wrapped in brown paper. Kate had painted a floral design and the girl's name on the plain paper. She handed the package to Jenny.

Jenny looked at Kate questioningly as she took the offered gift. She didn't speak, however, but carefully unwrapped the package, pulling off the tape without tearing the paper.

"Oh, Kate," she whispered. Tears filled her eyes. "You painted this for me?"

Kate's painting, a collage in watercolors, included Jenny in the right foreground as she looked now, Tim in the center as they both remembered him at the time of his death, and in the left background she had painted a younger Tim pushing his little sister on a swing.

Kate smiled, but her voice wobbled. "I wanted you to have something special to remember Tim by and to show you I still care. I hope this will help you get through your anger and pain, to have as a remembrance just for you."

Jenny gazed at the painting with a huge smile. "I know exactly where I'll hang it in my room. When you become a famous artist, I can say you painted this just for me." She put her arms around her. "Thank you so much, Kate."

"So, are you ready for the big day?" Ellie asked Jack.

"Almost." Jack put his hands in his pockets. "Mark and I will be moving my things into the apartment on Saturday. On Wednesday I'll open, and next Saturday will be the grand opening."

"Do you want us to deliver your arrangements on Wednesday or Saturday?"

"Wednesday, I think. We open at nine, so any time after that is fine. They should still look nice for Saturday, right?"

Ellie nodded. "They should be fine."

"Thanks, Ellie." He paid the florist for the two counter arrangements she would supply. He thought the flowers would make his new store look more inviting to customers.

As he started to leave, Ellie said, "I told Kate you were opening a store. She's doing well with her art, and her mom is feeling better."

Jack stopped and turned back. "Thanks for telling me, Ellie. I'm glad things are going well for her." He wanted to stay and talk about Kate, but Ellie had a business to run, and he had a lot of work to do today. Although Mark knew his plan to visit Mountain View after starting his business, he wasn't prepared to discuss it with Ellie. He left the shop with a to-do list on his mind, and Kate.

Jack took a deep breath as he headed for his store. Yesterday had been his last day at Clint's Computers. Clint shook his hand when he left. "I'm sorry to lose you as an employee, Jack, but I wish you the best with your business venture," He laid his hand on Jack's shoulder. "If there's something I can do to help you, let me know."

Jack knew he could count on his former boss if necessary. Clint was that kind of guy. "Thanks, Clint. I appreciate all I've learned from you. You took me in as a college graduate with only a little work experience."

He had planned to open in March. His opening had been delayed by about a month because of Blythe's death. Mark had returned to work after a couple of weeks, but both brothers found benefit working through grief with physical and mental labor. Jack depended on Mark's help, and he made sure his brother attended the grief group sessions.

The budding trees and flowers reminded Jack of Kate. He smiled when he remembered the old saying, "Spring, when a young man's heart turns to love." He loved Kate. He wished he could share this exciting time with her, his dream being fulfilled. She had her own life now, but maybe one day soon he could convince her to give him another chance.

CHAPTER TWELVE

Kate tried to attend every track meet at Mountain View High School that spring. Her talk with Jenny had helped free the girl from anger and bitterness. As her relationship with Jenny strengthened, she also connected with other students on the team. Some she knew from church, and some she didn't.

Pastor Michaels asked her to lead a Bible study for teen girls. "I've been watching you with Jenny and the other girls, Kate. You've connected with them. I'd like to capitalize on that. You have a knowledge of God's Word, and I believe you can help them grow as Christians," he said over the phone.

"I don't know. Do you really think I can?"

He chuckled. "You sound surprised. Yes, I believe you can. Tom and Emily Barrows have said how much you've helped Jenny. I've seen a difference, a new joy in her."

"May I have time to think and pray? Do I have to answer you right now?"

"Oh, I don't need an answer right now. Take time to pray. I thought a four-to-six-week study that will end before graduation would be good. My wife has some ideas for topics, or you may choose your own."

"Okay. I'll let you know in a couple of days." After ending the call, Kate blew out a breath. Teaching a Bible study for teen girls had never been in her plans. However, she enjoyed teaching the kids in the painting class. Maybe she should at least try.

Could she do this? She was excited about the opportunity but uncertain of her ability. Did she know enough about God and the Bible to teach others?

Kate walked back and forth in the living room and stopped before the window with her back to the room.

"Are you okay, Kate?" She turned as her mother entered the room.

Kate crossed her arms. "Yes, Mom. I'm okay. I just have a lot to think about."

Her mother said nothing more. Kate had never been chatty, and her mom knew she couldn't force her to talk when she wasn't ready.

Kate called Ellie and told her about the pastor's request.

"So, what's holding you back, girl? You know the girls, you have the time, and your pastor believes you can do it."

"I don't know, Ellie." Kate paced in her studio. "I think I remember what it was like to be a teenager. Sometimes it was hard. The girls struggle with some of the same problems I struggled with. A few of them are facing problems that I never imagined. What if I tell them something wrong or give them wrong advice? What if they ask a question I can't answer?"

"Then be honest. Ben and I have to do that with the young adults. We can't pretend to have all the answers. We have to be authentic and let them know we struggle with issues too."

Kate stopped pacing. "Then you think I can do it?"

"Yes, I do. You already have established yourself as their friend, so with plenty of prayer and study, it will work. However, it's a decision between you and God."

"I know." Kate plopped down on the loveseat and leaned back. "I've been praying a lot. I think Mom and Dad are becoming worried because I'm so quiet. I guess I should tell them what's going on and then call Pastor Michaels to tell him I'll do it."

"Good! Be sure to keep me posted about what happens."

"I will." Kate crossed her legs in front of her. "Thanks, Ellie. I needed to talk this out with somebody. You rescued me again. Every girl needs a friend like you."

Ellie laughed. "So, what are friends for?"

They finished the call, and Kate went upstairs to talk with her parents before calling Pastor Michaels.

AFTER SCHEDULING her appointment with Mr. Lake, Kate invited Jenny to go to Oakwood with her for her interview at the Four Seasons Gallery. That morning, Kate chose to wear a forest green linen shift with matching blazer and a simple gold chain around her neck. Her outfit made her feel professional and confident, almost. She wished the butterflies in her stomach would go away. Jenny seemed content to walk around the gallery, viewing the art while Kate had her interview.

As she shook hands with the man, he said, "Kate Greenway. I remember you now. You came in here often after we opened. We displayed some of your paintings in our high school shows."

Surprised that he remembered her, the young woman nodded. "Yes. Thank you for considering my work, Mr. Lake. I used to enjoy coming here, and I'm excited about the possibility of having you show my work again."

They sat down with a table between them. "Let's see what you have," he said cordially.

Kate clasped her hands together to keep her fingers still as Mr. Lake looked through her portfolio. He didn't speak, but he issued an occasional grunt or humph as he laid the paintings out before him. Kate wished for a place to wipe her sweaty palms and a cool cloth for her flushed face. She felt like a nervous teen on her first date. The thought made her smile.

He pursed his lips, then he looked at her. "These will do, Miss Greenway. You have real potential, and I'll be happy to add your paintings to our show."

Kate let out her breath. "Thank you, Mr. Lake."

"Now, I'll give you a folder with information about the show. You do realize other artists will be represented, and not all of them painters? We're showcasing local talent." Removing a folder from a file cabinet, he handed it to her.

Kate nodded. "Yes, sir." She opened the file and glanced through its contents.

He continued. "There will be a reception opening night for everybody, and then each of you will have your own time as well during the month your art is on display. You should read the contract carefully and ask if you have questions. The contract is our standard one and includes information on payments to you and our commission if your work sells. Think about how much you want for your paintings. I can give you guidelines for that." He handed her a brochure. "The price needs to be fair to the artist and attractive to the buyer."

Kate stared at the brochure in her hand, her throat tight with emotion. "Do you really think someone will buy my paintings?"

"Miss Greenway, I wouldn't be displaying your work if I didn't think it was sellable. Jonathan Weeks assured me there's a lot of interest in your paintings."

Kate inhaled a deep breath and let it out slowly as she tried to relax. "Thank you, Mr. Lake." She picked up the contract and the folder, along with her portfolio, shook hands with him, and went to find Jenny.

Jenny stared at her as she nearly floated out of the gallery.

"Are you all right, Kate? You look like you're going to do a ballet right in the middle of the sidewalk."

Kate laughed and threw her arms around the girl. "Oh, Jenny, yes! Mr. Lake is going to show my paintings! He likes them!"

"Of course, you're a good artist," Jenny said. Blythe used to say that too.

Kate skipped. "Thank you for coming with me today."

Jenny smiled at her and stood a little straighter. "That's okay. I liked looking at the art. Besides, you come to my track meets and cheer me on, like a real sister would."

Kate paused and looked thoughtfully at her friend for a moment. Yes, that's what Jenny had become, a younger sister. "Well, I'm glad you're here today to cheer for me." How she wished she could share this moment with Jack.

CHAPTER THIRTEEN

*K*ate missed the friend who had rescued her from wallowing in grief after Tim's death, and she missed working in the florist shop. She missed the meadow and the beautiful wildflowers growing there, and the little girl who listened to the blue spruce sing. She missed her other friends and the life she had created in Millvale. She would like to visit Blythe's grave, and, in spite of her best efforts to the contrary, she continued to think about Jack.

Blythe had kept her updated to a certain degree before her death, and Ellie mentioned him from time to time. Did he miss her at all? Would he ever change his mind about marriage? She hoped so, even if he married someone else, though her heart ached at the thought of him with another woman. Maybe, after her gallery show, she would take time for a visit to Millvale. If she timed it right, Jenny might like to go with her. But she had a lot of other things to deal with for now.

Although painting was her first love, Kate enjoyed working with flowers. If she had stayed in Millvale, she would probably still be working for Ellie. With spring's arrival, she decided to take time to get her mother's flower beds in order. It would be an appropriate Mothers' Day gift for her mom, who would be unable to do much gardening for a while.

"Dad, will you go with me to the garden shop this morning?" she asked on the first Saturday in May. Her mother was talking to Kevin on her cell phone in her bedroom.

He looked up from his laptop, where he had been working on a schedule of business appointments. "What are you up to?"

"I'm going to do Mom's flower beds as a Mothers' Day gift. I know she can't do them herself this year. I'd like your help carrying bags of fertilizer and mulch."

"In other words, you want me to provide muscle power and my pick-up." He smiled. "Sure, daughter, let's go. Let me tell your mom we have an errand to run."

He insisted on paying for the entire order. "You're putting in the labor, Katie, so this is my contribution. Having her flowers cared for will make your mother feel better, and gardening is not my forte." Kate allowed her father to pay. She would return at another time to buy more annuals to fill in the beds.

With her health improving, her mother had taken over most of the daily household tasks. This allowed Kate to plan her schedule so she could work outdoors for several evenings. Her mother came out to watch her, at times pulling a few weeds or making a suggestion from her lawn chair. Kate treasured the time with her mother, breathing a prayer of thanks that God gave them these moments together.

Maybe it was time for her to find a place of her own. Kate checked the real estate section of the newspaper for available apartments. Staying with her parents wasn't a problem, but she felt that all might benefit if she became more independent again. Mom didn't really need her there. If she moved into an apartment in Mountain View and remained available to help her mother, she could have her own place. Yet it was convenient having a studio in her parents' basement, close by any time of the day or night. Living with her parents for now didn't interfere with either her work or her ministry. However, her parents might prefer having the house to themselves again. She tossed the options around in her mind for a while before approaching them.

"I want to start paying you for staying here." Kate put up her hand when her father started to protest. "I need to do this or find an apartment. Mom doesn't really need my constant care, and I'm using your house and your food."

"You're welcome here, you know that," her mother said. "I enjoy having you, especially since your father is away so often."

"I'm beginning to make a little money now. I'm hoping to take on a few private students or classes. I may be able to sell some of my work at the gallery show. Maybe you and Dad can come up with what you consider a fair amount for me to pay you each month or each week, however you want to be paid."

"All right," Dad said, after a nod from his wife. "We'll talk about it and let you know."

UP UNTIL NOW, Kate had been so busy that she didn't realize how tired she had become. She woke up one morning at 6:30, checked her clock, and promptly fell back asleep. Two hours later her mother knocked on her bedroom door.

"Katie, are you all right? May I come in?"

Kate rolled over. "Sure, Mom," she said sleepily. Her eyes didn't want to stay open, and she struggled to remove the fuzziness from her brain.

"Do you realize what time it is? Don't you have an appointment with Mr. Lake to go over the gallery show contract?"

Kate grasped the clock on her bedside table. "Oh, no! I overslept! My appointment is at eleven o'clock, and I haven't even had my shower yet." She jumped out of bed.

"I'll have breakfast waiting when you're ready." Her mother backed out of the doorway.

"I don't have time for breakfast." She pulled a skirt and blouse from the closet.

"I'll keep it simple. You need to eat before you go." She shut the door.

Kate sighed. Moms will be moms. She didn't have time to argue.

Her day became worse when she had to rush back into the house for her copy of the contract. On her way to Oakwood, she noticed a red and blue flashing light in her rearview mirror. "Oh no!" She looked at the speedometer and hit her hand against the steering wheel. She pulled over to the side of the road and handed her license and car registration to the uniformed policeman who approached her open window. She tapped the steering wheel as she waited.

"You need to watch your speed, Ms. Greenway." He handed her the speeding ticket and returned her license and registration.

Kate's hand trembled. "Yes, I will, Officer." She put away her documents and checked her hot face in the rearview mirror. She waited for a couple of minutes after the policeman left to allow her nerves to settle.

Disgusted, embarrassed, and late, she greeted the security officer at the gallery door and knocked on the curator's open office door.

Mr. Lake looked up from his desk and stood. "Oh, Miss Greenway. You're late."

"I know." Kate stepped into the room. "I'm sorry, Mr. Lake, it has been a bad morning. I thought if I took the time to call you, I would be even later. I'm sorry to keep you waiting." Kate felt like a tardy school child.

"Well, you're here now. In the future, please call if you'll be late. I have another appointment in about twenty minutes. Please, be seated," he said cordially.

She sat down, feeling chastened but appreciating the fact he didn't belabor the point.

After going over the contract with her, and waiting while Kate signed two copies, Mr. Lake also signed them. He handed her a folded paper. "This is a list of artists and contact information. I thought it would be good for you to know something about the other artists whose work will be displayed and add them to your network."

They both stood. "Thank you, Mr. Lake." They shook hands. She took several posters advertising the art show to put up around Mountain View. She would send Ellie a couple of them to post in Millvale, maybe in the florist shop and the diner.

As she left the gallery, a busload of middle school students arrived. Kate nodded to the security guard as she went out the door. Behind her, Mr. Lake greeted the students, their teacher, and two parent chaperones.

The teacher looked familiar. Kate paused and looked back through the gallery's glass door. She saw that he was watching her as well. He smiled and waved, and she did the same. As she walked away, she searched her mind for a name or a reason to know this person.

Oakwood, larger than Mountain View, had more people and more businesses. Since it was her usual lunch time, Kate decided to try out one of Oakwood's restaurants. She chose Cathy's Café, just down the street from the gallery.

The small white tables and chairs accented the sage green walls and white woodwork, the décor both inviting and comfortable. Floral watercolors on the walls added to the garden-like atmosphere. Glass doors opened to a stone patio and a flower garden behind the café, where Kate could see more tables. The diners sitting at the tables, both indoors and out, looked contented, and delicious aromas wafted from the kitchen. Kate's stomach growled. The waiter and waitress, dressed in sage green and black, laughed and chatted with the patrons. Kate took a deep breath and relaxed, deciding she had chosen well.

The waitress approached her with a smile. "Welcome to

Cathy's Café. I'm Cathy. A table for one?" She led Kate to a small table against the wall. "If you would prefer, you may have a table on the patio." She handed Kate a menu.

"This is fine, thank you." If she liked the café, she would try the patio the next time.

"May I get you something to drink?"

"Just water, please. Your café is lovely, like a flower garden." Kate gestured with her hand.

Cathy's smile broadened. "Thank you. I told my husband I wanted a garden atmosphere, and I guess we succeeded. Would you like to order now, or do you need a little more time?"

"I think I need to look at the menu since I've never been here before. But if the food tastes as good as it smells, it must be delicious."

"Thank you. Our chef is great, so I think you'll be pleased with anything you order. I'll get your water for you."

Kate perused the menu. She decided on an apple-walnut chicken salad with house dressing. Cathy returned with a large glass of ice water and took her order. Kate, seated facing the patio, watched several couples and families enjoying their meals. The flowers made a lovely backdrop outdoors. As she examined the paintings on the walls, she imagined some of her own water-colors hanging in their place.

"Kate Greenway?" The male voice brought her suddenly out of her reverie.

Startled, she blinked at the man wearing the green waiter's shirt. "Sam?"

Kate pushed her chair back, and Sam leaned over to give her a hug. "It's good to see you, Kate. It has been a long time. I heard you had left Mountain View after . . ."

Kate nodded at Sam Pratt, Tim's best friend, who would have been Tim's best man. "I did leave for a while."

"So, have you moved back to Mountain View?" Sam pulled out the chair across from Kate and sat.

"My mom has cancer, so I came home to help out."

"Oh, I'm sorry to hear that. How is she?"

"She had a rough time for a while, but she's doing much better now."

"That's good news. What brings you to Oakwood?"

Just then Cathy brought Kate's salad. Sam stood up as Cathy placed the plate of food on the table. Kate's mouth watered at the aroma of the chicken.

"Kate, this is my wife, Cathy. This is her café." He put his arm around his wife and gave her a proud and loving look. "Cathy, honey, this is Kate Greenway."

Recognition dawned on the other woman's face, even though Kate was sure they had never met before. Cathy smiled. "Oh, yes." The smile was replaced by concern. "I was so sorry to hear about the death of your fiancé. I know Sam was devastated."

Kate experienced an unexpected surge of emotion and swallowed past a lump in her throat. "I had a difficult time," Kate told the couple. "God and friends got me through the hardest part. To answer your question, Sam, I'm in Oakwood today because I had an appointment with Mr. Lake at the Four Seasons Gallery. He's going to display some of my paintings."

"Well, congratulations! So you've continued with your art?"

"Sam, we have customers waiting. We'd better get back to work and let Kate eat."

Sam nodded at his wife. "See you later, Kate. Enjoy your lunch."

Kate smiled and gave a little wave, wishing the conversation could have continued. The food proved to be as tasty as the aroma promised. She'd have to recommend Cathy's Café to her friends and return herself. As she ate, she read over the list of artists and artisans to be included in the show. She recognized several names.

Oh! That's why the school teacher at the gallery looked familiar. He was Tim's pottery instructor. Kate had met him once. He and his wife ran a small pottery business. As with many artists and artisans, he probably had to supplement his income with a second job, at least until he became well-known as a potter.

She surely needed to supplement her income. The high school art teacher in Mountain View gave private lessons to the few people who wanted them. Her home town had only a sports center for youth and did not want to give Kate space to teach painting, as she had in Millvale at the community center. Mr. Lake already had a full schedule at the gallery, at least until after Christmas. Her fingers tapped the table top. Maybe she should look for work with a local florist. Another option would be to attend graduate school for her master's degree in education and teach art.

When she finished her meal, Sam brought her the check marked "paid." "It's on the house."

Kate stood. "Oh, thank you! Your wife has a nice place here. I'm going to recommend it to friends." They shared a side hug. "I'm glad we reconnected. I'll be sure to stop in again. How long have you been married?"

"I met Cathy soon after Tim died. We've been married almost a year. I have one more year of graduate school, and then I'll look for another job. Or maybe I'll stay here, and we'll expand. I like working with my wife."

"That's nice, Sam."

"When is your show, Kate? We'll want to attend."

"It begins on July 1. I wondered if you would display this poster about it." She handed him one of the posters from the gallery.

Sam looked at the poster. "Yes, I think Cathy will let us tape it to the front of the counter by the cash register. It's a local event and supports the arts."

With a lighter step she left the café. She looked up and down the street. Wayne had told her he managed a bookstore in

Oakwood. She saw the sign several shops up on the opposite side of the street. Checking her watch, she decided she didn't have the time to look him up that day. She liked to browse through bookstores, though. Next time she came to Oakwood, she would go there.

She mailed the posters to Ellie and called her that afternoon.

"I'm sorry we can't be there for opening night. Ben and I will be there the Saturday after the Fourth. We'll stay until Sunday afternoon."

"I understand, although I wish you could be here. I think I'll need some moral support."

"Nervous?"

"I'll say! My family will be here, of course. And friends from Mountain View."

"I will put up your posters. I can make more copies from the website. And Pastor Clary announced it from the pulpit."

"He did? Well, I can certainly use the prayer."

Did Jack know about the gallery show? She almost asked Ellie. Even if he did know about it, why would he come?

JACK LOCKED the front door of his computer store after his two employees left for the day. He gazed around with satisfaction. His decision to open a computer store in Millvale had been right. They'd had a lot of business at the time of high school graduation. Today they sold two computers and some accessories, performed three diagnostics, and several potential customers had come in to see the store and ask questions. Limited store space kept his stock of computers and accessories small. It wasn't a problem though, with on-line ordering and quick delivery. There would be room for expansion when it became financially feasible.

With Mark's financial investment and a small business loan

from the bank, he had bought a building on Main Street. The store was downstairs, and he lived upstairs. He went out the back door and locked it behind him, then climbed the outside stairs to his one- bedroom apartment.

The living room window looked out over Main Street. One of Kate's drawings of him and Blythe at the zoo hung on his wall. He lifted a photo of Kate from his end table.

In a few days he would visit her in Mountain View.

CHAPTER FOURTEEN

Kate didn't know what to do. Her mother's improved health left her unneeded at home. She had said goodbye to Tim and the past when she cleaned out the attic.

What did God have in mind for her? Using the Internet and social media, she explored some possibilities for her future. Even though the show at Four Seasons Gallery would give her wider exposure, she wondered if she should move to a city or to a place where she would have more opportunities for her artistic skills. Maybe she should return to Millvale to work for Ellie.

"Katie," her father said as they walked home from church, "your mom and I have discussed your proposal to pay room and board."

"Yes?" She held her breath.

Her mother spoke. "We want you to wait until September. That will give you a little more time to get your career started. We think it will be a way to help you, and we can never repay you for all you've given us."

Relieved to have a little more time, Kate breathed again. "You don't owe me a cent, but thanks." Although she had good intentions when she offered to pay rent, she still didn't have a regular, dependable income. Graduate school might be her best choice after all.

"Your mom has doctors' appointments and tests this week. We're hoping and praying for good news about the cancer." The look that passed between her parents spoke their love and hope. "By September we'll see how she is, and then we'll decide on payment. We'll see how your gallery show does as well."

Kate knew a lot depended on her mother's test results. Her father planned to accompany her mother for her appointments, taking several days off to do so. During her mother's battle with cancer, he had stayed home with her on particularly bad days, and he had taken her to see the doctor for regular updates once a month. Kate knew her mother's illness weighed heavily on her father's mind, and he struggled to remember God's love for them and His control over the matter. She knew there were days when her mother asked God why. Kate appreciated their transparency as they experienced their trial, never pretending that everything was all right, but choosing to allow God to grow their faith.

Kate's Bible study with teen girls ended just before high school graduation. She continued to attend a weekly Bible study for single young adults, which now included Wayne Quinn. She pretended not to notice how he often he sat near her, talked to her, and watched her.

While she wanted to be contented with her single state, a part of her longed to share her life with someone, the way her own parents shared with each other. In her heart, the desire for a family of her own remained strong. Even so, when Wayne asked her for a date, she said no. In reality, gray eyes did not measure up to blue ones.

She shared many things with her group of friends, although

she never told them about her relationship with Jack Chambers. Her feelings for him were too private and personal. A piece of her heart clung to the hope that Jack would change his mind. And she didn't want her disappointment to give them the wrong impression of him.

A couple from the group announced their engagement. Kate battled envy, and anger at Jack welled up in her. When she returned to Millvale for a visit, she would treat Jack just like any other person, pretending she had no special feelings for him. Maybe then she could survive. Maybe when she moved on with her life, she would find someone else. Maybe Wayne? No, she wouldn't lead Wayne on that way. She liked and respected him too much to make him think she wanted a relationship with him. He would make someone else a good husband. Besides, right now she didn't have time for romance. At least that's what she told herself.

As OPENING DATE at the gallery approached, Kate's tension increased. Several times she had to apologize for snapping at her mother. Too restless to spend much time in her studio, she did little painting. Hoping that something might jump-start her creativity, she never left the house without her sketch book in her quilted bag. She walked into the gift shop on the last day of June and noticed the absence of a certain miniature of Blythe in the meadow. "Did someone buy the miniature of the little girl picking wildflowers?" she asked Jonathan Weeks.

Jonathan handed her a check for the paintings that had been sold recently. She looked at it, pleased with the amount she had received. "Now that tourist season is beginning and people are traveling, a lot of people are stopping in. Your paintings are getting a great deal of attention. I sold a couple just yesterday. I make sure to point out the poster for the show at Four Seasons."

"Thank you, Jonathan. This money will help a lot."

Jonathan smiled. "I'm glad to help. You're one of Mountain View's own. It's good for my business too." He gestured with his hand. "You asked about the miniature. A man just bought it. Said something about knowing the artist."

"Oh." Kate looked around. "He knows me? Did he give his name?"

Behind her a familiar voice said, "Jack Chambers."

Kate spun around to find Jack grinning at her. Her mouth fell open, her heart flip-flopped, her knees nearly buckled, but she managed to say, "Jack, I . . . I didn't expect to see you here!"

When Jack reached out his hand to her, she grabbed it, glad for the support.

"We need to talk," he murmured. When Kate nodded mutely, he asked, "Is there some place we can go?"

Kate attempted to unscramble her thoughts. "There's a park down the street. We can go there." Remembering Jonathan, she turned back to him. "I'll be back."

With a grin on his face, he gave a little wave. "Don't hurry on my account." He walked across the shop to help a customer.

She pulled her hand from Jack's before stepping out of the shop. Why was Jack here? What would they say? Did she want him here? Should she have introduced Jonathan to him? Her mind raced, her thoughts jumbled. The bell on the door jingled behind them.

With Jack beside her, her heart thumping, Kate directed her steps to the park, conscious of the curious stares of passers-by. Kate's was a familiar face in Mountain View, and a stranger roused interest. The couple settled on a bench in the middle of the small park, angled away from the sidewalk and street, beside the rose garden. A row of shrubbery gave them a little privacy.

The roses, now in bloom, filled the air with their fragrance. Kate sat with her knees slanted toward Jack, so he wouldn't sit too close, and she could watch his face. She waited, her body rigid, detecting a purpose in the man before her.

JACK CLASPED and unclasped his hands as he looked around him and collected his thoughts. He knew it was up to him to explain his presence in Mountain View. He ran his fingers through his hair and wondered how to start the conversation.

"How is your mother?" Ellie had kept the church in Millvale updated on Claire Greenway, but he wanted to show Kate his personal concern.

"Mom is doing well now. She had a tough battle with the cancer, and she's waiting for the results of a couple of recent tests."

Relieved that she would talk to him, he said, "I know it must have been a tough time for you too, Kate. I'm sorry I haven't been here for you." She said nothing. Jack continued. "You probably heard I've started my business." She wore her hair longer now and pulled back into a pony tail. Her gaze challenged him. He rubbed his hands on his legs. "It took longer than I had anticipated, and my plans were on hold for a while after Blythe left us."

Kate touched his hand. The strong desire to grab her hand and hold on made Jack pause. He took a deep breath before continuing. "I opened three months ago, and I'm doing okay. But I've been trying to come up with a business logo and wonder if you'll help me create one."

As though he had come all the way to Mountain View to ask her to create a business logo.

"Well. I . . ." Kate stuttered at the unexpected request.

"It's all right. I understand if you don't want to do it." It was a stalling tactic anyway until he could work up the courage to say what he had come to say.

"No, no, it's not that. You surprised me. Advertising graphics is not one of my strengths. I'll try if you let me know what you want." Knowing Kate, she probably had designs and colors already swirling around in her head.

"Thank you, Kate. Mark suggested it, and I thought between your artistic skill and my computer skill, we could create something good. We'll talk about it later. I've taken a room at the Bellemont Bed and Breakfast, and I'm planning to stay until after the Fourth." He watched for her reaction to his plan.

Her eyes widened. "Oh, you are?" At least she didn't demand that he leave today.

Before she said any more, Jack handed her a package wrapped in pink paper. Kate bit her lip, and she hesitated before accepting it. "I promised to deliver this to you."

Kate held the gift as the quacking of ducks on the pond drew her attention. Both she and Jack turned to look when a childish voice cried out, "Look at the ducks, Mommy!" The blonde preschooler giggled as she and her mother tossed pieces of bread to the ducks, who gobbled them hungrily.

Kate glanced at Jack and found him watching her, waiting expectantly. Carefully she turned the package and released the tape. Pulling the paper apart, she gasped. "Oh, Jack, it's—"

"—Blythe's painting." Jack finished for her. He moved closer and placed his arm around Kate's shoulders, pleased when she didn't pull away.

Kate leaned into Jack's embrace. She bit her lip as tears spilled over and trailed down her cheeks. She gazed at the child's framed picture. From a flower-filled meadow bordered by blue spruce trees, a girl climbed a rainbow toward puffy, white clouds, waving to a shining figure at the top.

"It's beautiful! So much like Blythe. Look at the color and detail. She was a true artist, Jack." For several minutes the two of them examined the watercolor by the little girl they both had loved. "Did Blythe know she was going to die?"

Jack removed his arm from Kate and rubbed his hand against his pant leg. "I wondered if she did. She often talked about her mother and heaven. I think she tried to prepare us." Jack wiped his tears. "She seemed to be getting stronger, then she was gone."

"She told me she thought her mother was happy in heaven with Jesus." Her eyes searched Jack's face. "How is Mark?"

Jack gazed at the roses and swallowed before answering. "My brother's pain was so great at first, I think he wanted to die, to join Rachael and Blythe in heaven. I really worried about him for the first couple of weeks. He's doing better now. He's had grief counseling, and he joined a bereavement support group. He's still traveling a long, hard road." Jack choked up. He blinked rapidly, his eyes on the ducks.

"And you, Jack?" she asked softly, touching his hand again.

He grasped her hand with his before she could withdraw it and held it tightly. He took a deep breath and finally looked at her. Tears stood in his eyes. "I miss her so much. She was like a light, a flame to brighten the world. She gave us so much joy." Jack paused and looked deeply into Kate's eyes. "She brought us together." He angled himself toward her. "How about you, Katie? How are you doing?" He saw himself reflected in her eyes.

She looked down at their clasped hands. "Dad didn't get home until after the time of the funeral, and Mom was so sick at the time, I couldn't leave. I wanted to say goodbye to her."

"I thought you might have returned to Millvale by now. Didn't Ellie save your job for you?"

Kate inspected Blythe's gift again. "I was afraid, Jack. I didn't know whether I would be welcome, even though Ellie had a place for me." Jack avoided her gaze by pretending interest in the roses. He understood her meaning. She didn't know that he had watched for her to return to Millvale. "I'm here at least until September. And now that my paintings are selling, I'm fulfilling a dream. God has blessed me more than I could imagine. Did you know I'm going to have a gallery show?" Jack heard the excitement in her voice.

"I hope I'm invited." Jack brushed Kate's cheek with his fingers.

Kate's eyes widened. He captured her gaze with his. His eyes flickered to her lips. He wondered if she would let him kiss her. She laid the painting between them on the seat and looked away. When she found her voice again, she nodded and said, "Of course. It opens tomorrow evening."

"Will you allow me to escort you to opening night?"

"You want to go with me?"

Jack chuckled at her astonished expression. "Like a date. Why wouldn't I want to go with you? It would be my pleasure and honor." His smile faded. "Unless there's someone else."

Kate looked around as though remembering they were in the park, a public place. She pushed a stray hair behind her ear and said, "No, there's no one else, and yes, I'd like to have you go with me."

He took a deep breath and released it. He set the painting on her other side and slid closer. He held her hand against his chest. "I have missed you so much, Kate. I kept waiting for you to come back. I looked for you."

He searched her face when she remained speechless, wishing he could read her mind. He continued, rubbing his thumb against the back of her hand. "My heart broke when Blythe died. But when I think about her, I realize how much I would have missed if she had never been born, or if I had never known her. I watched you recover from Tim's death and go on with your life. Even though Mark is going through a lot of pain, he doesn't regret having loved his wife and child. He can still thank God for the time he had with them. I have a lot to learn, Kate. Will you help me? Can we try again?"

She turned her hand to intertwine her fingers with his. "This isn't a good place. Wow! What are you saying?" She trembled.

Jack clasped her hand between both of his hands. "I know I hurt you, and I'm sorry. I have been selfish. Will you forgive me?"

She rubbed the back of his hand with her fingertips, sending a current up his arm. "I had decided we were done, that friendship was all I could expect from you." She looked over his shoulder, then at him. Two tears escaped her eyes and ran down her cheeks. "Yes, Jack, I forgive you."

"After you left Millvale, I tried to forget you, but I expected to see you everywhere. I waited for you to appear. Blythe kept asking when you would be back. Mark scolded me, calling me a fool for letting you go. He's my big brother. I guess I should listen to him." He gave her a smile. "I want to get to know you better, to go forward with our relationship."

His eyes locked with hers.

Jack took a deep breath. "I love you, Kate. I don't want to lose you. I want us to have a future together."

She brushed a lock of hair off his forehead. "I love you, too, Jack."

He heaved a big sigh. "Thank you, Kate." He raised her hand to his lips. He smiled, his gaze moving to her mouth. He heard her intake of breath. Remembering their public surroundings just in time, he decided he needed a distraction. He raised his gaze to her eyes and said, "Do you think Blythe is clapping her hands up in heaven? She did all she could to keep us together." They laughed together, breaking the intensity of the moment.

Kate slid Blythe's painting, protected by the pink paper, into her bag. Then she stood and held out her hands to Jack. "Please come home with me. My parents will be happy to meet Blythe's uncle Jack."

He took her hands and stood. "I want to meet them too. I'm serious about my relationship with you, and I want them to know

I'll be hanging around." He couldn't imagine his life without her. "Then maybe you'll let me take you out to dinner tonight. Sort of a pre-show celebration."

Kate squeezed his hands. "That sounds nice, Jack." She cleared her throat. "My brother and his family will be here for the Fourth. You'll get to meet them too."

"Your big brother?" Jack asked, pretending to chew his nails. "What have you told him about me? I've heard about big brothers. How protective is he of his little sister?"

"Oh, very," Kate warned. "You'll have to pass the inspection of both my father and my big brother."

"Big brothers can be intimidating. I should know."

Laughing, they left the park hand-in-hand. Jack, relieved that Kate would give him a second chance, felt as though he floated with his head in the clouds.

CHAPTER FIFTEEN

The whole night sparkled, like the stars twinkling overhead. Kate wondered if her happiness made her sparkle. She had carefully chosen her dress, of aqua lightweight satin with cap sleeves and a mandarin collar, for this special night. She looked across the room to where he stood talking with Mr. Lake. Jack caught her gaze and winked at her. She blushed.

Still recovering from the shock of his unexpected arrival and declaration yesterday, her thoughts wandered to the possibilities of their future together. She never expected she'd be this happy again. Although she had hoped for Jack to change his mind, she had doubted its probability.

A voice interrupted her reverie. "You have a glow about you tonight, Kate. I understand that young man talking to Mr. Lake is with you," said a smiling Emily Barrows.

Kate nodded. "So, you've met Jack? I hoped you would meet him. He's from Millvale."

"You've been keeping him a secret," she teased.

"Let's just say that God sometimes works mysteriously to perform miracles, I didn't expect him to visit me in Mountain View."

Emily nodded. "I see. Well, I think congratulations are in order in more ways than one. This show is wonderful, and your paintings are beautiful. What a lovely dress!"

"Thank you. And thank you so much for coming tonight. It means a lot to me."

"We owe you for helping our daughter." Tom Barrows joined his wife. "Jenny is like a new person. She has not only overcome the emotional difficulty caused by Tim's death, but her faith has grown." Tom placed a kiss on Kate's cheek. "Have you tasted the hors d'oeuvres, Emily? They melt in your mouth."

"No, I haven't tried the food. I've been appreciating the art." She took her husband's arm.

"I don't know if you realize," Kate said, "but there's a café down the street that serves wonderful food. I suggested to Mr. Lake that Cathy's Café could cater this show. You might be interested to know that Cathy is Sam Pratt's wife."

The Barrows both looked at Kate. "Tim's friend Sam? We haven't seen him since the funeral," Emily said.

"Yes, Sam is helping his wife in the café while he finishes graduate school. I met him one day when I had lunch there. I think they hired some waiters to serve here tonight, but they were going to try to come."

"Well, we'll have to be sure to stop in at the café soon. It would be good to see Sam." The Barrows walked away as Kate's father approached. She looked around for Jenny. She hadn't seen her for quite a while. She waved to her mother, seated and talking with someone Kate didn't know.

"I'm so proud of you, Kate. We both are," her father said, putting his arm around her shoulders. "I'm not sure if your glow is from the excitement of the show or from your beautiful dress or from the presence of a certain young man. Or is it a combination of all of the above?"

"Thank you, Dad. You and Mom have been such an encouragement to me."

"Your mom and I both like Jack. We think you've made a good choice, and so has he."

Kate pushed a stray hair back from her face. "It was so unexpected. I kept hoping, but I didn't believe Jack would change his mind. Sometimes I can hardly believe he's here."

Paul kissed his daughter's forehead. "Your mother is getting tired, so we're going home. We've had an exciting few days, and I don't want her getting sick. I'm sure Jack will take care of you." Her father joined her mother, and the two of them left.

Kate had just decided she needed a drink to quench her thirst when Jack appeared at her side with two glasses of punch. "For my beautiful girlfriend," he said with a smile, handing one to her.

"Oh, thank you so much. I'm parched. How did you know I needed this?" She sipped the cold, refreshing punch.

Jack smiled. "I saw you looking toward the punch bowl and licking your lips. You have been talking to a lot of people, so I figured you needed a drink for your dry throat. Do you want anything to eat? The hors d'oeuvres are very good."

"No, I'm too excited to eat." She walked to a bench and sat down with a sigh. Her feet ached.

Jack joined her. "Do you think your feet will touch the ground tonight?" He put his arm around Kate's shoulders and pulled her close.

Kate scanned the room, looking at the people and at her art hanging on the wall. She looked at Jack, and she shook her head. "Probably never," she whispered with another sigh.

Mr. Lake, accompanied by a middle-aged couple, approached them. "Miss Greenway, may I present José and Nikki Santos. They are interested in purchasing some of your paintings, and they wanted to meet the artist."

They stood, and Kate shook hands with the couple, noticing the custom cut of his black suit and the perfect fit of her black sheath. "This is my friend, Jack Chambers." Kate became aware of Jack's arm resting comfortably around her waist.

José Santos smiled at her. "Miss Greenway, it is a pleasure to meet such a talented young artist. Mr. Lake has outdone himself in his collection of art here tonight. I think this display alone says a great deal for our region."

"Thank you so much, Mr. Santos. Please, call me Kate. It is an exciting evening for me, and I appreciate that Mr. Lake has included my paintings in this show."

"And please call us by our given names, Nikki and José."

Nikki Santos then spoke. "I'm a pediatrician, and I'm looking for paintings for the walls in my waiting and examination rooms. I love the painting of the little girl playing in the meadow. You have somehow captured the child's spirit."

Kate smiled and glanced at Jack. "She's Jack's niece, Blythe. She was a wonderful subject, so easy to capture on canvas."

"How delightful! Her name fits her well."

Kate nodded, and Jack's arm tightened around her. "Blythe passed away a few months ago of respiratory complications. We all miss her."

"I'm so sorry." She laid her hand on Kate's arm and looked at Jack. "But how wonderful you captured her in your paintings. A couple of your acrylics would fit very well in my office."

As they examined and discussed Kate's paintings, Jack stepped back so Kate could move closer to the prospective buyers.

"I'm interested in a couple of your landscapes of this area. They will be just right for my real estate office," José said. "You live in Mountain View, correct?"

"Yes, I do."

"Do you do commission work?"

"I haven't yet, but I am interested."

"I know several business associates who might be very interested in your work. You bring out the beauty of our region, a good way to promote tourism and business."

Kate took a deep breath, glanced at Jack, and then said to them, "Thank you so much, both of you. Your support is encouraging to me." She shook their hands. Mr. Lake escorted the couple to his office to discuss business details.

Many of the guests had left, so Kate and Jack walked through the other rooms in the gallery, stopping to speak with the other artists and artisans, surprised at the variety and quality of the art, from sculpture, wood carvings, and wood furniture, to quilting, batiks, and pottery.

"I feel humbled by seeing all this." Kate gestured with her hand. "I never realized I grew up around such great talent."

"Look," Jack said, pointing. "There's a pottery display. I'd like to see it. Remember the verse from the Bible you shared with me?"

Pleased that Jack remembered, Kate nodded. She introduced Jack to Tim's pottery teacher. "Jack, this is Henry Nickles. He teaches pottery, and he and his wife have a business a few miles from here."

"Ah, yes, Kate Greenway, isn't it?" Henry said, shaking their hands. "You were just coming out of the gallery when I arrived with my class of young art appreciators a while back."

"You looked familiar, but it took me a few minutes to realize why I knew you. A friend of mine, Tim Barrows, took classes from you." Kate glanced at Jack, hoping he didn't mind another reference to Tim.

"I remember him because he enjoyed making pottery so much. I appreciated his enthusiasm. By the way," he said, taking the hand of the young woman next to him and pulling her close, "this is my wife and partner, Lily."

Jack and Kate shook hands with her. "It's nice to meet you." Kate waved her hand at the pottery display. "Your pottery is gorgeous! I wish you lots of success."

They talked with Henry and Lily for a few minutes then went on to see more. Kate tried to figure if she would be able to afford to buy the lovely green vase in the Nickles' display. She knew her mother would love it. She sighed and shook her head.

Jack squeezed her hand. "Is something wrong?"

"No, not really wrong. I'm an artist and want to make a living from my art. It's just that art can be so expensive. Not that it's not worth it, just hard to pass up when you can't afford it."

"Is there something back there you wanted?"

"Well, yes, for my mother. Did you notice the small green vase?"

Jack nodded. "It caught my eye too. Maybe after you sell some of your paintings, you'll be able to buy the vase."

"Maybe," Kate responded. "Just think, Henry and Lily can take lumps of clay and make such beautiful objects."

Jack squeezed her hand." Isaiah compares us to lumps of clay, which God makes into something of value to Himself—us. I understand now why Tim enjoyed making pottery."

They continued around the gallery until they arrived back in the room with Kate's paintings. They sat on the bench to rest.

"At Blythe's funeral, Pastor Clary talked about masterpieces of the Father's creation. You know Ephesians 2:10?"

Kate quoted, "For we are his workmanship, created in Christ Jesus for good works, which God prepared beforehand that we should walk in them."

"Pastor Clary said that 'workmanship' can be translated 'masterpieces.' In God's sight, we are all masterpieces of His creation when we know Christ as Savior. No matter how long or short our lives, He planned for us to do good works by living in obedience to Him." He paused. "I was so angry at God for taking away people I loved. I felt He just wasted people by allowing them to die too young."

"And now?" Kate prodded. A new painting took form in her mind, of a potter and clay.

"Now I understand that Blythe, Rachael, and my parents were all God's masterpieces. Their lives were not wasted, and they are with the Savior in Heaven. God is still working on us, still working to make us something better to glorify Him." Jack gazed into her eyes. "I know I'm better because He brought you into my life."

Mr. Lake approached them before Kate could respond, and he told her about the sale of her art. "I would say we had a successful opening night. Several hundred guests have been through tonight, and we have the potential of selling a great deal of the art on display." Mr. Lake rubbed his hands together.

"You have the heart of an artist and the eye of a businessman, Mr. Lake," Kate said.

"It's kind of you to say so, Miss Greenway. For me the greatest benefit is getting to meet young artists and encouraging their careers. It's a vision my wife and I had for the gallery."

"Then I believe you are a success, sir," Jack added. "Although my skill lies in appreciating art rather than creating it, I thoroughly enjoyed the experience of being here tonight."

"It was good meeting you, Mr. Chambers." They shook hands, and Mr. Lake moved away.

Kate waved when she saw the Barrows family leaving. They waved back, except for Jenny, who pushed out the door without looking at her. Earlier, the girl had bubbled over with excitement and thrown her arms around Kate. She exclaimed about the exhibits and the people. Later Jenny talked with Jack by the refreshment table, her hands gesturing. Kate then noticed a change in her young friend. A veil of coldness replaced the exuberance. Jenny displayed the same attitude toward her before their talk about Tim. She would make it a priority to visit Jenny tomorrow.

The museum closed at 11:00 p.m. As Jack pulled out of the parking lot, Kate relaxed against the seat and yawned. "I'm glad you're my driver. I'm tired."

Jack raised his eyebrows. "That's the only reason you're glad?"

"No, silly. What I mean is, I'm so tired, I'm not sure it would be safe for me to drive."

"What else are you glad for?"

"I'm glad for the show, and I'm glad you came to be with me."

"Me too." Jack's hand found hers, and their fingers intertwined.

The warmth of his touch traveled up her arm to her heart and gave her butterflies in her stomach. The shock caused by Jack's sudden appearance and declaration of love still lingered. She could not express the delight of his presence with her tonight, at one of the most exciting events of her life. The months of separation and little hope made her appreciate his presence even more. She remembered Mark's words. "Be patient, Kate. He'll come around. Once he finally makes up his mind, he won't change it again." She counted on Mark being right.

As she thought about the events of the evening, she remembered that she wanted to speak to Jack about Jenny. "Jack, I saw you talking to Jenny Barrows tonight."

"Jenny? Oh, I remember. Tim's sister. The pretty girl wearing the gray skirt and pink blouse."

"Yes."

"We started talking. She reminded me a little of Blythe, she was so excited about being there."

"I know what you mean. She was very excited to be there. When I had my meeting with Mr. Lake, to show him my portfolio, I brought Jenny with me, so I think she felt she had a part in this whole thing."

"It was strange, though," Jack mused. "I guess she recognized me from your drawings or paintings as Blythe's uncle. She seemed to get suspicious, and when I told her I had come to the show with you, the change was like day and night. She apparently lost interest in talking to me and walked away. I never saw her smile again the whole evening, although I saw her studying you a few times."

"I was afraid of that." She paused a moment and gazed out the window into the night. "Jenny had a difficult time accepting Tim's death. She nearly worshiped her big brother. When he died, she became angry and clung to the anger. Her mother asked if I could help Jenny, so we talked, and I've spent a lot of time with her, as her friend. It was hard for her to understand how I could go on with my life if I had really loved Tim. She finally opened herself to allow God to heal her hurt. If she knows about us, I may have to do some damage control tomorrow."

This was a troubling glitch in an otherwise wonderful day. *God, please give me wisdom to deal with this right.*

Kate yawned again as Jack pulled up in front of the Greenway home just after midnight. He turned off the car and leaned across the seat toward her.

"Did I ever tell you how beautiful you are?" His kiss took her breath away. "And talented and sweet and beautiful?"

Kate giggled. "I think you said that twice." Her hand cupped his cheek. "Did I ever tell you how grateful I am that you are here with me tonight?" He shook his head. "Well, I am. I have been triply blessed by God tonight. You're here, my mom is getting better, and my painting career is getting a jump start. I love you, Jack Chambers."

"I love you back." They shared a second kiss, sweet, tender, memorable.

She broke away first. "I think I'd better go in now, Jack. We'll have all day tomorrow."

He formed a pout with his mouth. "You do have to be practical." He smiled. "Oh, well, you're right. I don't want to have to answer to your parents for keeping you out too late." He got out of the car and came around to open the passenger door for Kate.

As they walked to the house, she said, "We're not teenagers, Jack. And I don't have a curfew."

"I know, but I wouldn't want them to worry. I've never dealt with the parents of the woman I love before."

They stood by the front door, facing each other, reluctant to say goodnight. Her parents had left the porch light on.

She laid a hand against his chest. "Jack, I hope you don't mind hearing so much about Tim. I felt like I kept saying his name tonight, and so did a lot of other people."

He held both her hands against his chest. "At first I felt uncomfortable. Then I realized this is his territory, where he grew up, and people knew him."

"Tim was my first love. He'll always have a place in my heart. But I love you now, Jack. I hope you'll never feel threatened by my memories." She searched his face.

He leaned forward and kissed her gently. "You are one special woman, Kate Greenway."

Relieved, Kate said, "Why don't you plan to come over for breakfast in the morning?"

"Thought you'd never ask. What time?"

"No earlier than 7:00," she said with a smile. "Probably 7:30 would be good."

"Oh," Jack said, "not 5:30?"

"No way! I need time to get my beauty rest, and so do you."

Jack pulled her close. "I'm not sure I'll sleep much tonight." They kissed again, and he stepped back as Kate opened the door and slipped inside. She turned and blew him a kiss. "Me neither."

She closed the door and leaned against it for a moment, breathless and filled with joy. She walked over to the living room window and pulled back the curtain to watch Jack. He stopped at his car door and searched for her. When he saw her, he smiled and blew a kiss. Kate waved back. He got into the car and drove away. Kate snapped off the lights and went to her room.

CHAPTER SIXTEEN

Sleep eluded Kate for a while. When she fell asleep, she didn't wake up until 6:45 in the morning. She had forgotten to set the alarm, and Jack would soon be there. She had to rush through her morning routine. At 7:30 she answered the door with her feet bare and her hair still damp from her shower.

His blue gaze captured her. He smiled in response to her smile. "Good morning, beautiful. I would have brought you flowers, but the shops aren't open yet."

When he stepped in, she closed the door and put her arms around his neck. Their lips met in a sweet kiss, then Kate snuggled against Jack, held in his arms. They may have stood there longer if they hadn't heard a loud "Ahem!" from the living room doorway.

They jumped and pulled apart, laughing. Kate's father, trying to sound severe, said, "So we have an early morning visitor." He stood with his arms crossed in front of him. His attempt to look grim failed. The corners of his mouth twitched.

Jack stepped forward and extended his hand, which Kate's father clasped. "Yes, sir. Good morning."

Kate spoke up. "I invited Jack to come for breakfast, Dad. I'm fixing it."

"Well, I'll make sure your mother knows. Since you have everything under control, I'll go about my business."

"Whew!" Jack exclaimed softly after he left.

"Don't worry about Dad. He knows we won't break any house rules. He and my mother have given you their seal of approval." Kate started for the kitchen. "I hope you like what I'm fixing."

"Don't worry about me," he said, following her. "I'm easy to please when it comes to food, and I'm sure whatever you make will be delicious."

"I hope your confidence isn't disappointed, although my cooking skills have improved tremendously over the past couple of years. My mom's cooking is hard to beat. I think she has missed doing it." Kate took ingredients from the refrigerator and cupboard and placed them on the counter. "My family likes waffles for a special breakfast."

Jack stood behind her. "Mmm, sounds good." He wrapped his arms around her waist and rested his chin on her shoulder. "I don't know how I ever thought I could live without you." He nuzzled her hair. "You smell nice."

Kate savored the embrace and words, still amazed by his open show of affection. She leaned back. "Jack, will you get the waffle iron down for me?"

"Sure," he said, still holding her

"Jack?" Kate turned her head to look at him.

He smiled and kissed her nose. "Now, where is that waffle iron?" She pointed, and he reached it easily.

They worked together comfortably. By the time her parents came into the kitchen half an hour later, they had the table set, and they had nearly finished making the waffles. Kate decided to have a family breakfast at the kitchen table. When her brother and his family came tomorrow, they would have to move into the dining room.

"What time do you expect Kevin and Lindy tomorrow?" Kate asked her mother.

"They'll be here in the afternoon, before suppertime," her mother replied. "They're all looking forward to meeting Jack, especially Cody and Melissa."

"I'm looking forward to meeting the rest of Kate's family," he said. "She talked about all of you when she lived in Millvale."

"We've certainly been glad to have her here to help out for the last few months. Our daughter is one special person. She gave up a lot to come back to Mountain View," Dad said.

Her mother nodded her agreement.

"God has been so good to me." Kate's hand found Jack's under the table. "I believe coming back here was the right choice for several reasons." Jack squeezed her hand.

After they finished the meal, Jack and Kate sent her parents out of the kitchen while they cleaned up.

"I have to go see Jenny this morning. Will you be all right staying here with my mom and dad for about an hour? I think it would be better for me to go alone, until I find out why she left angry last night."

"Oh, I don't know." Jack clasped his hands and hunched his shoulders. "Do you think it's safe to leave me here alone with them?"

"Silly!" She kissed his cheek. How she enjoyed this relaxed and teasing Jack. When she left the house a few minutes later, Jack and her father were sitting in the living room discussing Jack's business.

She parked in front of the Barrows' home, walked up to the door, and rang the bell, wondering what she would say. Jenny opened the door, dressed in blue shorts and a green tee shirt.

"Hi." She didn't meet Kate's gaze.

"Hi, Jenny. I think we should talk." A direct approach would be best.

Jenny nodded and stepped out on the porch, closing the door behind her. Kate sat on the porch swing, and patted the seat beside her, inviting the girl to sit next to her.

"Did you have a good time last night?" Kate asked.

"I guess," Jenny answered. She twisted a lock of hair.

Kate pushed with her feet to rock the swing. "Jenny, you were so excited about the show, until you found out Jack came with me." She looked directly at the girl. "You know who he is?"

"Yes," said Jenny in almost a whisper. "He's the guy in your pictures, the little girl's uncle."

"And why did it upset you to meet him? Did he do or say something to you?"

"It's not him. It's you," Jenny said, refusing to look at Kate.

"Me? What did I—?"

Jenny stood and faced her. "You're leaving again, aren't you? You're going away with him!"

"Jenny, I . . ." Kate didn't know what to say. "I'm sorry, Jenny. Who told you that?"

"I'm not a baby! I saw how you looked at each other, the way you and Tim used to!"

Kate licked her lips as she thought for a moment. "You're right, Jenny. You're not a baby. So, I'll talk straight to you. Jack is my friend. You are my friend. I don't have plans to leave here right now. That doesn't mean I'll stay in Mountain View forever. Probably you won't either."

"Are you going to marry him?"

"Jack hasn't asked me to yet. I care deeply about you, Jenny. You're a dear friend. If Jack does propose, and we get married, I want you to be happy for me."

Jenny finally looked at her, tears in her eyes. "I'm sorry, Kate." She sniffed. "I'm sorry, but I don't want you to go away again." Deflated, she plopped down on the swing. "Acting grown-up isn't always easy."

Kate laid her hand on the girl's shoulder. "Life always brings change, Jenny. You're changing and growing up. When you're ready for college or marriage, do you want your parents to say, 'No, you can't, we want you to stay here with us?" Jenny shook her head. "Do you think it's fair to force me to stay here if God wants me to go somewhere else?" Jenny shook her head again, pulling a lock of hair across her lips. "Maybe, while Jack is here, you can get to know him better."

"Jack's nice, and I'm sorry I was such a grouch. Will you forgive me, Kate?"

"Of course. Remember, we're friends. It doesn't matter where either of us lives, we'll still be friends. Okay?" She nudged the girl with her elbow.

"Yes. Thank you, Kate." The teen threw her arms around her. She sat back and pushed with her foot to get the swing moving again. "Remember when you told me to let go of my anger at my brother's killer?"

Kate nodded. "I remember," she said, wondering why Jenny brought up the subject at this time. Their discussion about it had taken place more than two months ago.

"I've been thinking. I want to write a letter to the man in prison and tell him I forgive him."

"What gave you that idea?" she asked softly, trying not to show her surprise.

"I read about it in a book. I want him to know that I forgive him, and it's the only way I can think of to let him know. Don't you think it's a good idea?" Jenny's tone of voice begged for her approval.

Kate watched a sparrow as it perched on the porch rail and flew off. "If you want to do it, talk to your parents first. They can help you find out how to do it. It may help both you and him."

"I think he meant it when he said he was sorry for what he

did to Tim. Maybe when I tell him I forgive him, I can tell him about Jesus' forgiveness too."

Kate cupped the teen's cheek with her palm. "You're one special person, Jenny Barrows. Your brother would be proud of you." Jenny's expression showed her pleasure at Kate's words. "You have the mark of the Master Craftsman on you. You're growing up just fine." They rocked together in silence. "Next week, when I have my night at the Four Seasons Gallery, would you like to go with me?"

Jenny bounced in the seat. "Oh, I'd love to go! I'll have to ask my parents though."

"Of course, there's plenty of time. Jack has to go back to Millvale after the Fourth, so maybe you and I can make it an event, go out to eat beforehand. I know a lovely café." Kate remembered the crush thirteen-year-old Jenny had had on Sam. She thought seeing Sam again would be fun for her friend and maybe for Sam, too.

"Thanks, Kate."

When Kate arrived home, she found her mother in the kitchen starting lunch preparations. She heard the men's voices from the living room.

"Hi, Mom," she said, approaching from behind and resting her chin on her mother's shoulder. She reached over and snatched a grape, popping it into her mouth.

"Now, Katie, don't spoil your lunch," Mom teased. Then she added, "It feels so good to be able to putter in my kitchen again. To be able to smell food without getting sick."

"I know, Mom. And it's good to see you in here again. Not that I mind cooking. I'm beginning to enjoy it. But what you make tastes so good!"

"Thank you, dear. Compliments bring rewards." She popped another grape into her daughter's mouth. "How did your visit with Jenny go?"

"Good. I think we've come to an understanding." Mom

raised her eyebrows at her daughter's choice of words. "Really, we're good," Kate assured her.

Mom nodded. "I'll fix lunch. Now, maybe you should go in the living room and rescue Jack." She gestured with her head in response to a loud moan.

"Checkers?"

"He challenged your father."

"Oh, no! I'd better rescue him." Kate never knew anyone who could beat her father at checkers, although Kevin had come close a few times.

Her mother smiled as she nodded her agreement.

Jack looked up when Kate entered the living room. "Hi, guys!" She perched on the arm of the chair where Jack sat opposite her dad at the checker board.

Jack groaned and held his head. "How did I ever get myself into this?"

"I should have warned you about Dad and checkers," she said, patting his shoulder.

Her father looked at her with a twinkle in his eye and a smile on his lips. "Hi, Katie!" Kate was sure he was up to something. He jumped the remainder of Jack's checkers with his.

Jack conceded his defeat. He put his checkers back in the can then stood and stretched. Kate helped him push the chair back into place. "Good game, Mr. Greenway, but you should have warned me. I thought I was a good checkers player."

"I learned from my dad, who was the best in his day." Dad grinned at him. "If you two have plans, go ahead."

"Mom's puttering in the kitchen, and she said she'll fix lunch. Want to take a walk, Jack?" Kate held out her hand.

"Sounds like a plan." Jack entwined his fingers with hers.

"We'll be back in time for lunch. I want to show Jack more of Mountain View," Kate told her father.

Dad, still smiling, waved them away as he picked up the checker board and put it away.

The day promised to be hot, but a gentle breeze kept the heat bearable. They stopped at the gift shop to see if any more paintings had been sold, then they sat watching the ducks in the park for a while.

"How did your talk with Jenny go?" Jack asked, rubbing his thumb across the back of her hand.

"Good. She thought I'd be moving away again. We agreed that life holds many changes, and she didn't have the right to force me to stay here always. I told her friends remain friends, even if they move away."

"She thought I'd take you away from her?"

"Yes, she did. Her own observations led her to that conclusion." Kate glanced at her companion to measure his reaction. He just smiled. "But I think we worked out the problem. I'd like for you to get to know her better, if there's time."

Jack rubbed her cheek with his knuckle. "I think that's a great idea." He leaned toward her and said, "You know, you should have warned me that your father's a checkers pro."

"Maybe." She giggled. "And ruin his fun? No way!" She tilted her head. "I guess you found plenty to talk about while I went to see Jenny?"

Jack shrugged. "Oh, we discussed this 'n that. Shall we go out for dinner tonight? I saw a nice restaurant over in Oakwood."

He changed the subject so quickly, Kate became suspicious of a conspiracy between Jack and her father. What were they up to?

"Yes, I'd like that. Oakwood has several nice restaurants." Kate stood. "Shall we continue our walk?"

They arrived home in time for lunch. Afterwards, Mom needed a nap, and Dad had some business to take care of.

After her father went out the back door, Kate turned to Jack. "How about we call Jenny and invite her to go for ice cream with us? I want her to get to know you better. And I think she has something to tell you."

Jack grabbed her hands. "As long as I can hang out with you, it's fine with me, my dear."

Kate wondered at the change in Jack. The tension most often present between them in Millvale had been replaced by delight in being together. Jack's wall had disintegrated.

They met the girl at the ice cream shop and walked to the park to eat their cones. When Kate and Jack joined hands, Jenny scooted to his other side.

"I'm sorry I was such a jerk at the gallery last night, Jack."

"I accept your apology, Jenny. I'm glad we can be friends." He glanced at her. "Kate tells me you're a track star."

Jenny smiled and blushed. "Well, not exactly a star, but I like to run, and I'm improving my time. Kate cheered me on at every home meet this year."

"Jenny has been my cheerleader at the art gallery." Kate gave her young friend a thumbs-up.

"May I join this mutual encouragement society?" Jack asked.

"Sure!" they said together. Jack joined them as they gave a thumbs-up.

Relief and joy filled Kate's heart as she witnessed a bond form between Jack and Jenny.

CHAPTER SEVENTEEN

Another sparkling night, although Jack seemed restless. He played with the silverware, turned his water glass around and around, and tapped the table with his fingers. Kate noticed but didn't comment. They ate their meal accompanied by quiet conversation. Their eyes met often in the soft candle light.

When they finished eating, he said, "I saw a garden out back, Kate. Would you care to take a walk?"

Kate folded her napkin and laid it beside her plate. "Yes, I saw it too. A walk would be lovely." Romantic, actually. Kate stood and smoothed the soft folds of her cranberry red sleeveless dress.

Tiny white lights illuminated the way as they strolled along the garden path.

Warm, humid night air held the fragrance of flowers. They stopped to rest on a white, wrought iron garden seat. Jack lowered himself on one knee on the ground in front of Kate. She almost stopped breathing.

"Kate Greenway, I love you. I want to be with you always. Will you marry me?"

Kate reached out to touch her beloved's face. It took her a

moment to be capable of speech. "Jack, I—Oh, Jack, yes!" How often she had longed to hear those very words.

He reached into the pocket of his blazer and withdrew a small, black velvet box, which he opened to reveal a diamond ring. Kate's breath caught as he took her left hand and placed the ring on her finger before leaning forward to kiss her. She put her arms around his neck and returned the kiss. For a breathless moment they seemed like the only people in the world. They pulled apart when they heard voices coming toward them. Quickly Jack sat next to her, and they smiled and nodded at the couple who walked by. Kate watched as they disappeared along the path.

Jack leaned toward her. "When do you want to get married?" he asked, his breath tickling her ear. When she turned her face toward him, he kissed her nose.

"Did you have a date in mind?" She held up her hand, trying to get the diamond facets to catch the dim light.

"How about tomorrow?"

She put her hand in her lap and giggled. "I think we might have to wait a little longer than that."

"Will it have to be a long engagement?"

"Not too long," she promised. "Why don't we talk about it tomorrow? We can tell my parents tonight, and you should call Mark." She laid her head against his shoulder. "I didn't know you'd ask me so soon, if at all. I'm still a little befuddled."

He put his arm around her. "Really, Kate, I wasted so much time with you by resisting my true feelings for you when you lived in Millvale. I had several long talks with God, and I went to Pastor Clary for counsel. I came here prepared to ask you, but I thought you might refuse me. I knew you had good reason to." He smiled into her eyes. "Your father and your mother gave their permission this morning."

She pulled back slightly. "That's what you and Dad were up to! I knew something was going on."

Jack chuckled and kissed her again. He stood. "We'd better go. We don't want to get your parents out of bed, and I want to have time to call my brother."

When he tugged gently on her hand, she stood. Arm in arm, they walked slowly down the path and back to the car.

The night sparkled, like the stars in the sky and the ring on her finger. Even the fireflies sparkled as they winked among the shrubbery. She wished this night could go on forever.

She could hear Ellie saying, "You go, girl!" And Blythe clapping her hands for joy.

"I TALKED to my brother last night." Jack sat on the love seat in her studio, leafing through her drawings of Millvale. Most of them made him smile.

Kate, dressed in her smock and holding her palette of acrylics, stopped painting to ask, "What did he have to say?"

Jack paused, gazing at the drawing of him blowing bubbles with Blythe. He remembered that day—the day he knew he loved Kate. "Would you have time to make a painting of this for me?"

Kate looked at the picture then at her fiancé. Jack clenched his jaw as he fought for control of his emotions. She put down her paints and brush and sat next to him, laying her head on his shoulder. "That was a special day."

He kissed her hair, inhaling the floral scent. "I knew I loved you that day, but I refused to commit myself." He touched the face of the little girl in the sketch. "Did you know that the first day we met you, Blythe decided I should marry you?"

When Kate shook her head, he continued. "Yes, she did." He leaned his head against hers. "She was right, you know."

"Yes," Kate agreed. "I miss her, too, Jack."

"On the phone, my brother said, 'It's about time you came to your senses!' To you he sends his love and best wishes. He can't wait to have you for a sister-in-law. He said he's sure Blythe is leading the cheering section in Heaven."

Kate brushed a black speck from the drawing. "I'm sure." She laid her hand over Jack's. "If you want me to do a painting for you, Jack, of course I will. You and Blythe are my favorite subjects. Can you wait until after next week?"

"Yes, there's no rush."

They sat quietly for a few more minutes, Jack's mind on the new possibilities in their relationship and the wonder of loving this woman. After a few more moments Kate stood. "I have a little more to do on this painting today, then we can discuss the wedding if you want to." She painted a few more strokes.

"October. Can we set the date for October? Is that too soon?" Jack asked.

Kate smiled. She leaned over and kissed his lips. "I think October will be all right. My pastor will want to do pre-marital counseling. We'll have to meet several times with him, and he'll make us read some books. They're helpful too."

"I guess we'll have to call him and set up a meeting, maybe before I leave day after tomorrow. I wondered if you wanted to get married here or in Millvale, but I think you'd prefer Mountain View."

Kate dipped her brush in the paint. "It will be easier for Mom, and this is my home church. I'd like to ask Jenny and Alanna to be bridesmaids and Ellie to be my matron of honor. And I hope you'll agree to let my niece and nephew have a part too."

"Of course. I'll ask Mark to be my best man. I might also ask Ben and your brother to stand up with me."

"There's a calendar hanging on the wall over there." She pointed with her brush toward the stairs. "Why don't you get it, and we'll choose a date? Alana is somewhere in the world, so I hope she'll be able to be here. If not, I'll ask Lindy to be my third attendant." She made a few more strokes with her brush. "I'm done here." She put away her paints and washed out her brushes.

"Mark said something else." Jack removed the calendar from the wall and sat again. "He suggested that we live in the cottage, and he would move to the apartment above my business. He doesn't want to sell the house yet, but sometimes the memories are overwhelming for him. He thinks a change might help."

"Live in the Three Bears Cottage?" Kate removed her smock. "I think I'd like that, as long as you agree and it's best for Mark."

"We have a few weeks to decide." Jack turned to October on the calendar.

They called the pastor to set up an appointment for July 5, before Jack left Mountain View. Right after lunch they went grocery shopping for her mother. They walked around town while they waited for Kevin and his family to arrive.

"I want to show you something, Kate." Jack pulled out his wallet and removed a photo. He handed it to her. The frayed edges and a fold on one corner attested to much handling. A man and woman with two boys smiled from the picture. She recognized the boys.

"These are your parents, with Mark and you." She handed it back to him. "They look wonderful. You must have been a happy family."

Jack examined the photo for a moment. He returned it to his wallet, which he slid back into his pocket. "We were. My mom and dad had the same kind of relationship your parents have. And the same kind I want for us. They always took time for us, and every week they went out on a date by themselves." Jack took her hand and squeezed it. "Mom would have liked to have daughters-in-law. She said it would be nice to have a girl in the family. Mark has the family photo albums. You should see them."

Kate laid her free hand on his arm. "I'd like that, Jack. I think your mom and dad must have been special people because of what I see in their sons. Their legacy shines through both of you."

Jack gazed into her eyes. "Thank you, Katie. Your words mean a lot," he said, his voice gravelly with emotion. He liked being compared to his father, a man he had admired and loved. He only hoped he could live up to his legacy as a husband and father.

A horn honked as her brother's tan minivan passed by. Four hands waved, and they waved back.

"Come on, Jack" Kate urged, tugging his hand. "Race you back home!" She took off, and he followed. Just before arriving at the Greenway house, he put on a burst of speed and passed her. They arrived, breathless and laughing, to greet Kevin, Lindy, Cody, and Melissa as they got out of the van.

Jack's palms began to sweat, and he sighed inwardly as Kate made introductions. Kevin's handshake and words showed his approval and relieved some of Jack's anxiety.

"It's good to meet you, Jack. My kids have been talking about you. It seems they saw some pictures in Kate's studio at Christmas." He grinned and added. "We wondered what kept my little sister in Millvale so long."

His little sister gave him a playful push.

"Have you set a date yet?" Lindy asked as they greeted one another.

Kate nodded. "Yes, October 21."

Melissa tugged on her tee-shirt. "Aunt Kate?" Kate bent over when her niece crooked her finger. "Is Jack your boyfriend now?" she asked just loud enough so everyone could hear.

Kate peeked at Jack, smiled, and hugged her. "Yes, sweetie, he is. In fact, we're going to get married, and we want you to be the flower girl."

The little girl clapped her hands and jumped up and down. "Oh, goody!"

Cody pulled himself up to his full height. "I'm Cody. I'm almost nine." He shook hands with Jack.

"Pleased to meet you, Cody. Your aunt Kate said you play baseball."

"I love to play!"

"My brother and I used to be in Little League, and we played ball in high school. Maybe we can have a game of catch after dinner." He looked at Kevin for approval. Kevin nodded.

Kate's parents joined them outside, and there were more excited greetings. Taking advantage of all the offers to help, Kate's brother had the minivan unloaded in no time.

Jack became quiet. As he watched the chattering, happy people around him, Kate's family, his own family memories flashed before him. Kate nudged him. "Are you okay?" she asked. They remained outside while the others went in.

Jack put his left hand in his pocket. With his other hand he grasped hers and led her to a more secluded place on the lawn, behind some shrubbery. Turning toward her, he wrapped his arms around her. "Just hold me a minute, okay?"

Putting her arms around his waist, she rested her head on his chest. He tightened his arms around her. She waited for him to speak.

When he spoke, his voice rumbled in her ear. "When you told me about your family, Kate, I never realized what it would be like. Mark and I never had a big family. After our parents . . ." Jack swallowed. "After our parents died, it was just us, except for Uncle Harold. Then after Rachael died, it was us and Blythe. Now it's just us again. But when you and I get married, I'll belong to a family bigger than I ever had. I never knew how much I missed." He trembled, took a deep breath, and stepped back. "I feel doubly rewarded because you said yes." He kissed her gently. "So blessed."

When they joined Kate's family in the house, Kate's mother looked at them, her forehead furrowed with concern. Jack placed his arm around her shoulder and leaned toward her ear. "Everything's fine."

Her face smoothed out. She kissed his cheek and joined the rest of the family. He touched his cheek, remembering his own mother's kisses from long ago. As Kate slipped up beside him, he took a deep breath and let it out slowly. It was as though he had been welcomed home.

The excited chatter quieted as they found their seats around the dining room table for the evening meal. Paul's mealtime prayer included thanksgiving for love and family and for his wife's healing. The noise level rose again as they ate Claire's delicious lasagna. Jack agreed. Kate's mother made exceptional food.

The Greenways readily accepted him as a family member, including him in conversation and teasing. He thought it would be harder to get to know them, but he had already fallen in love with Kate's family. While they enjoyed dessert, Jack stood up and cleared his throat. They all stopped talking and eating as they looked at him.

His body trembled with emotion. "I'm not sure how to begin. I have only my brother, Mark. My family has always been small. My parents died years ago. Mark lost both his wife and daughter." Kate reached out and took his hand. "I didn't know when I finally realized I couldn't live without Kate," he looked at her, "and what having a family again really meant. I told Kate I'm truly blessed because she said yes. I'm getting a wonderful, beautiful wife." There were nods and murmurs of agreement. "But I'm also getting the privilege of being part of a wonderful family. Thank you for . . ." Jack couldn't continue, so he sat, face toward his lap, tears running down his cheeks.

Kate rubbed his back, and someone passed him a tissue. Silence reigned except for numerous sniffs. Suddenly Jack heard the sound of a chair being pushed back, and light footsteps ran toward him. A small, soft hand caressed his cheek, two arms surrounded his neck, and a sweet voice said, "It's okay, Uncle Jack. We want you to be in our family. We have lots of room."

Jack turned and pulled Melissa into his lap, holding her close. The Greenway family all got up and gathered around him, touching him, comforting him with words. Paul led his family in prayer.

The day she left Millvale, Kate had warned Jack he would be lonely without love. He had walled up his heart to close friendships, except for Mark and Blythe, and the young artist had broken through his protective wall. Jack had not recognized his loneliness until Kate left.

Now he would marry the woman he loved and belong to a loving, caring family.

CHAPTER EIGHTEEN

Kate couldn't say what she ate for breakfast. Ever since seeing Jack after her arrival in Millvale last night, uneasiness plagued her. As soon as he greeted her, she knew something was wrong. His embrace and kiss had been warm and affectionate, filled with longing. He had teased Jenny, who had accompanied her on the long drive. Kate knew him well enough, however, to detect a problem. Had she said or done something to upset him? She couldn't think of anything.

Everything was falling into place. Jack had returned to Mountain View twice, to meet with Pastor Michaels for pre-marital counseling, and their wedding plans were coming together. Why couldn't she shake the feeling that something was wrong?

Jenny entered the kitchen with Ellie. "Have fun with Jack. I'm off with Ellie to Mill Valley Florist," she said with a dramatic accent and pose.

Turning from the sink where she had been gazing out the window and washing the breakfast dishes for Ellie, Kate dried her hands and hugged her young friend. "I'm sure you'll have fun. Thank you, Ellie, for letting her go with you this morning. Make sure you keep her busy and out of trouble."

Ellie laughed when Jenny made a face at Kate. "I think I can manage that. Jenny and I get along quite well." She waited while the girl went out and closed the back door behind her. "Is everything okay, Katie? You seem a little bit distracted this morning."

Kate shrugged. "Just pre-wedding jitters, I guess. I'm okay." She wanted to talk to her friend, but she had to talk to Jack first. Instead she said, "You look wonderful this morning. You wear prospective motherhood well." Ellie and Ben had announced the news of a baby expected in the spring. "I appreciate that you're letting both Jenny and me stay with you."

"What are friends for, girl? Well, don't worry about Jenny. Have a good time with Jack." She paused with her car key in her hand. "You said you would visit the cemetery today?"

Kate nodded. "Jack agreed to take me. He knew I wanted to go. I know it's hard for him." She bit her lip. "Millvale isn't quite the same without Blythe."

"I'm glad you have each other to lean on now." Ellie squeezed her friend's arm. "See ya." Ellie went out, and Kate heard the car start.

Leaving the dishes to dry in the drainer, she brushed her teeth and hair, checked her clothes, and took one last look in the mirror. She made sure she had her sketch book and the spare front door key Ellie had given her and slung her quilted bag to her shoulder. The thought of seeing Jack in just a few minutes excited her and filled her with unease.

She closed the front door behind her and sat on the step to wait for him. The wail of a siren, an answering dog's howl, the slam of a door, and a car starting broke into the stillness. She waved to a neighbor backing out of his driveway.

The morning air held a slight chill. Kate shivered and pulled her sweater around her. August would soon end and September begin. Only eight weeks until their wedding. She ticked off in her mind what still needed to be accomplished before that day arrived. Today they planned to visit the cemetery and talk with Mark about the cottage, and Jack would show her his business and apartment.

She breathed deeply, trying to calm her worry. Why didn't Jack come or call? Her chest tightened, her heart beat faster, as her mind returned to another time someone had been late—the night Tim died. She nearly gasped for breath.

Just as she took out her phone to call him, he pulled up in the driveway. Relieved but still a little angry, she rose and brushed off her jeans. As she walked toward the car, she took a deep breath and blew it out, trying to slow her heart rate and dispel the anger. Jack greeted her with a smile and a kiss and opened the car door for her. She slid in, buckled her seatbelt, and leaned back in the seat with her eyes closed.

Jack got in the driver's seat and closed his door. She heard the click of his seat belt. "Is everything okay, Kate honey?" he asked. "Are you not feeling well?"

"Yes. No!" she answered, shaking her head. "You were late, Jack. I almost had a panic attack, I think. I wish you had called when you knew you would be late."

"I wouldn't stand you up, Katie. I had to stop at my store for a few minutes, and I met Ben on the way out. I had something I wanted to ask him. I'm sorry, I should have called. I didn't realize you would worry. Forgive me?"

Kate stared straight ahead. "The night Tim died, he was late. All I could think of was the same had happened to you."

Jack released his seat belt and leaned over, gently turning her face toward him. He caressed her cheek with his thumb. "I'm so sorry, honey. I never even thought about that. I'll try not to do that to you again." He wiped tears from her face with his thumb and kissed her.

She grasped his hand. "I know there will be times you won't

be able to call, and this hasn't happened before. I don't know why I panicked, except last night . . ."

"What?"

"There was something bothering you last night, wasn't there? You didn't say so, but I thought maybe you were having second thoughts."

Jack paused for a moment, his jaw working. He took a deep breath. "I was."

Kate's eyes widened, and she gasped.

"Not about marrying you. I want to spend the rest of my life with you," he hurried to assure her.

"What then?" she demanded, anxiety making her voice sharp.

He leaned back in his seat. "About having children, becoming a father. We're going to talk to Pastor Michaels about that at our next session."

"You don't want children?" She thought they had agreed to having at least two. She didn't know how to respond to this unexpected wrinkle.

Her breath caught at the tender expression in his eyes when he looked at her. How she loved him.

"That's why I wanted to talk to Ben, to get his perspective. He agreed that the idea of being a father, of being responsible for a new life, can be overwhelming. But we have to believe God is always there for us. He prayed with me, and I think I'm okay now."

"Are you sure, Jack? I want this settled before the wedding. I don't want to fight about having children after we're married." She shook her head. "I thought you had taken care of your old fears."

Jack rested his chin on the steering wheel. "Last night when you came, all I kept thinking was, 'What if you knew about my doubts and I lost you?'" He turned his head and took her hand. "Don't you ever wonder, Kate, about how you'll handle problems in the future, or kids?" His eyes searched her face.

Kate nodded. "Yes, especially you." She smiled when his mouth opened and snapped shut. They both laughed. The tension between them dissolved. "We'll succeed if we stick together, Jack, and trust the Lord together."

A little fear remained in her mind, however. She loved him so much and never wanted anything to come between them.

Jack refastened his seatbelt and started the car. He paused and looked at her. "I love you so much. I wish we could get married tomorrow, but I guess we need a little more time to iron out some wrinkles."

They leaned toward each other, their lips connecting in a kiss before he backed out of the driveway.

"Mark said he'd meet us at the cottage for lunch. He's going to stop at the deli and pick up some subs. He would like to be there when you go through his house, even though I could show you everything."

"That's okay. It's his house. I'm so touched that he's giving us the option to live there."

"As a big brother, Mark is the best. He's excited for us. I don't think I can ever repay him for all he's done for me."

"I don't imagine he expects payment, does he?"

"No, I guess not." He stopped at an intersection and waited for a car pass by. "Do you want to visit Blythe first or go to see my store?"

Kate thought for a moment. "Why don't we stop at Ellie's and get some flowers? We can go to the cemetery first. That way, if you go to your store and have to take care of a business matter, we won't feel as pressured."

At Mill Valley Florist, they found Jenny helping Ellie arrange a new shipment of mums in an array of autumn colors. She greeted them cheerfully. As they tried to make up their minds what to purchase, they witnessed the teen's animated manner with a customer. Jenny seemed in her element. Ellie, at the front counter waiting on another customer, looked over her shoulder at them and smiled.

"How about these nasturtiums, Jack?" Kate asked.

"Is that what they are?" He touched one of the blooms. "They are pretty."

"What do think of buying these for now, and after the wedding, we can buy some mums?"

They purchased the pot of flowers from Ellie, and they took a few minutes to talk to Jenny before leaving for the cemetery.

They pulled up near Blythe's gravestone. Although no other person appeared, they saw another car parked a short distance away. They approached quietly, hand-in-hand. Jack carried the pot of flowers in one arm. Kneeling together, Kate brushed some yellow leaves from before the gravestone while Jack placed the flowers to the side. She rubbed her hand gently over the small stone and traced the name and dates. Jack's arm came around her, and she leaned against him, suddenly overwhelmed with grief. She had already mourned Blythe's passing and knew she was in a better place, but how she missed the little girl! As she cried, she felt Jack's trembling. Her arm encircled his neck, and they let their tears fall unashamedly, drawn together by their sorrow.

Kate had come supplied with a pocketful of tissues. She handed some to Jack. They stood, and Jack pointed out Rachael's grave beside her daughter's. A mini-rose bush, planted between the two simple gray stones, displayed a profusion of bright crimson roses.

"Rachael loved roses. She loved flowers, and she had a green thumb." As Jack spoke, Kate remembered the flower gardens at the cottage. "Mark plants a rose here every spring. The cemetery association insists that we make sure dead flowers are taken away, and we have to remove everything before the snow falls, or they'll mow them over." At her surprised look, he added, "It sounds heartless, but it keeps the place neat and easier to care for. They close the gates to cars during the winter, although we're allowed to walk in. Mark is careful to follow the rules. Our flowers will be fine here," he assured her as they walked back to the car. Kate nodded, feeling at peace after the storm of tears.

They stopped at Jack's store, where Jack introduced her to his two employees and showed her around. No in-shop emergencies delayed them. They climbed the stairs to look through Jack's small but modern apartment above the store. They agreed they could be comfortable here, although Kate wondered where she would paint.

"Do you think you'll want to work in my store?"

She shrugged. "I don't know a lot about computers, honey, but I suppose I could fill in when you really need the help. Maybe the cash register." As they left the apartment and walked back down the stairs, she added, "I thought I might work with Ellie again, at least part time. When she has her baby, she'll need someone to help in the shop. Will that be all right with you? A lot will depend on how much I paint."

"I know painting is your priority, and you liked working with Ellie. It's fine with me. You'll be in Millvale as my wife. We'll be together. I'll be content with that," he promised.

In the meadow, the blue spruce gently waved their branches in greeting. The grass had been allowed to grow tall, and bright, golden black-eyed Susans and white Queen Anne's lace had replaced earlier flowers. The weathered picnic table stood near the trees, and the swing swayed back and forth in the breeze.

"The meadow has been neglected this year," Jack confessed. "We haven't had the heart to do anything here since Blythe died. To be honest, Katie, it was so lonely here without you even before that. Blythe and I both waited for you to come back. Maybe next year we'll use it again."

Kate sighed, "Yes, next year." The meadow song whispered in the trees.

CHAPTER NINETEEN

Mark welcomed Kate with a bear hug, leaving her almost unable to breathe. The dining room table had been set for lunch.

"It's good to see you, Kate! You too, Jack," he said, clapping his brother's shoulder. "I'm glad you finally took your big brother's advice and asked her to marry you." He spoke to Jack while grinning at Kate. Jack grimaced.

Mark's face showed signs of strain, thinner and paler than Kate remembered. She touched his arm. "It's good to see you, too, Mark. How are you doing?"

Mark's grin vanished. "I've struggled, Kate. At first I felt as though I had lost my reason for living. It was hard to accept God's goodness and love after He allowed my little girl to die."

His jaw trembled, and he turned away for a moment. "God never let me go, however. This brother of mine didn't either." He turned back and laid a hand on Jack's shoulder. "He kept checking up on me, and he encouraged me to get help. The grief still hits hard at times, but I'm managing to go on."

Kate knew what he meant. She understood grief.

"Why don't you two have a seat at the table?" Mark suggested. "Everything's ready. I just have to get it out." Kate offered to help. "No, I can do it, but thanks anyway."

He brought in a platter of cold cuts and rolls for sandwiches, a small tray of vegetables with dip, a bowl of potato chips, and a pitcher of iced tea. He said the blessing, and they passed the food around.

"I decided to get the fixings rather than subs," he explained. "I thought we should eat first, then I'll show you around, and we can talk about what Jack and I have discussed."

"We both appreciate your offer to let us live here," Kate said.

Mark finished making his sandwich and looked around the dining room. He gestured with his hand. "I love this house. Rachael made it our home. I've spent the best part of my life here." He poured himself a glass of tea. "Sometimes the memories are overpowering." He paused. "I don't want to sell it, and the thought of strangers moving in is almost unbearable. Giving you the option to live here seems the best solution. I know you two will take care of it, and the apartment will help me get away until the memories don't hurt so much. Besides, the house is so empty with just me." He stopped and cleared his throat before biting into his sandwich.

Kate looked at Jack. The corners of his mouth turned up, and he squeezed her hand under the table. As they finished lunch, they discussed the show at the Four Seasons Gallery, Kate's family, and wedding preparations. Disposable plates, cups, and utensils made clean-up simple.

Mark led them on a tour of the cottage, mostly for Kate's benefit. Although Kate had spent much time with Blythe outdoors, she had never been farther than the kitchen and half-bath inside. The charming cottage was decorated country-style, the rooms small. The door to Blythe's room stood open. Kate paused in the doorway. The room had been cleaned, but Blythe's paintings hung on the wall. Child-sized, pink, fuzzy slippers sat on the floor beside the small bed covered with a ruffled, quilted, pink bedspread. Her children's Bible lay on the table next to the bed. A place of memories, where a father remembered his beloved daughter. She bit her lip and wiped tears from her eyes. Jack squeezed her hand.

❧

"THERE'S a surprise for you out back, honey," Jack said. He had remained quiet during much of the tour. He enjoyed watching Kate's reaction to the house, his second home. His love and desire for her grew each day as they approached their wedding date. They could start their marriage and their family while living here. Their family? The sudden thought startled him. He really did want children together with Kate.

Mark led them out the back door. "You know Rachael was an artist."

"Yes." Kate chuckled. "That was one of the first things Blythe told me."

"Well, she painted as a hobby only." He pointed to a small white building with green shutters and door. "This was her studio. After she died, I turned it into a workshop of sorts. Sometimes Blythe and I came out here together."

He unlocked and opened the door. He stood back so Kate could step in first. Jack entered behind her and put his arms around her. She leaned against him.

"I asked Mark if you could use it as a studio for your painting," Jack said. "It's insulated and heated. It just needs to be cleaned up a little bit." Some jars of paint stood on a shelf, and a few tools and pieces of wood and paper lay on the workbench.

Kate walked around as she examined the studio. "I'm overwhelmed. It's perfect! You guys are so thoughtful. For some reason," she said, turning her head to look at Mark beside them,

"I get the idea you really want us to move in here, and you're sure this will convince me."

"Now, Kate," Mark said with a smirk, "I don't want you to feel pressured."

From behind her, Jack added, "This feature does add to its desirability."

Mark chuckled. "Now you sound like Mary Jo King, Jack."

"Mary Jo King? Who is she?" Kate turned around to face Jack.

Jack rolled his eyes upward. "Just the real estate agent who helped me find the building for my business." His ears became hot.

"Oh?" Kate cocked her head, her eyebrows raised.

Grinning at his brother's reaction, Mark explained, "She was very interested in my little brother in high school. She's an aggressive sort of woman."

"To say the least," Jack muttered. Kate grinned. She obviously enjoyed this exchange between him and his brother.

Mark cleared his throat, the corners of his mouth twitching. "Anyway, that's a line she uses frequently when showing real estate. She's good at her business. But, I assure you, she couldn't catch Jack. You are his one and only romantic interest."

"That's good." Kate smiled at Jack and patted his cheek. If Mark hadn't been present, he would have kissed her.

She walked around the small building. "The windows let in a lot of natural light." She picked up a scrap of wood from the workbench and rubbed her fingers over it. "I think this will do very well."

She set the wood down and turned toward Jack. When her eyes connected with his, he knew she wanted it. She nodded at him.

"See, I said it would make the property more desirable. Kate and I would like to live here, Mark. We'll work out the details before the wedding."

"Sounds good."

∼

WHEN THEY RETURNED to the cottage, Mark brought out the family photo albums, and the brothers explained the photos to Kate. Jack did most of the talking, opening up about their parents and his childhood. She better understood Jack's loss and felt closer to him.

Later that afternoon they spent some time with Jenny, stopping for ice cream and walking around the town. They met Ellie, Ben, and Mark at Mill Pond Diner for the evening meal. As she stepped into the diner, Kate's thoughts returned to that evening, it seemed like eons ago, when a small girl and her uncle had invited her to their table and into their lives, and they had found a place in her heart.

The young ducks on the Mill Pond, as big as their parents now, would soon be migrating, flying away to a warmer wintering place, and Kate would return to Millvale to stay. When the ducks came back in the spring, she would be here to witness the wonder of new life and growth and moving on. Always change, yet somehow the same. Always moving on, yet remembering where they had been.

She squeezed Jack's hand as the group made their way to a table in the dining room. When he squeezed back, she wondered if he had similar thoughts. She could hardly wait to return to Millvale, to experience the wonder of her new life as Mrs. Jack Chambers.

∼

MRS. MATTHEWS MADE a bee-line for them the next morning in church. She drew Kate into a warm embrace. She greeted Jenny with, "Welcome, my dear," and a hug, and touched

Jack's arm. "I knew you were meant for each other. I prayed and prayed."

Jack surprised both Kate and Mrs. Matthews when he put his arm around the shoulders of the older woman. "I have you to thank for this? It's your fault that I saw the error of my ways and asked Kate to marry me? And she said yes?"

Mrs. Matthews chuckled. "I guess you can say that. Someone had to do it. Prayer and love never fail."

Kate listened in stunned silence to their banter. Jack threw back his head and laughed. He winked at her.

"Mr. Matthews and I will be in Mountain View for your wedding, Lord willing. I've waited too long to see this boy married to miss the occasion." She turned to Jenny and said, "Now, my dear, how would you like to meet my grandson? And his sisters, of course. They're visiting before school starts."

Jenny looked at them, grinned, and shrugged. "Sure," she said and walked away with the talkative woman.

"Always the matchmaker," Kate commented.

Ellie and Ben had a cookout that afternoon, inviting several other couples from church to join them.

The telephone rang. Ellie answered it and then approached Kate.

"Cindy Matthews, Mrs. Matthews' granddaughter, is on the phone. She wants to know if Jenny can go on a hike this afternoon with her family."

Kate thought for a moment. "Why not? Jenny should be okay with them, and she'd probably like spending some time with kids her own age for a while."

"I thought maybe the attraction might be the grandson," Ellie said with a smile.

"That's true. But they'll be chaperoned, and I trust Jenny. Why don't you let Jenny talk with Cindy?"

The afternoon passed quickly. Jenny returned from the hike,

bubbling with excitement and a little dreamy-eyed. After evening worship, they went out for pizza with several friends from church. Kate suggested Jenny invite her new friends to keep her company.

ELLIE INVITED Jack to come for breakfast the next morning. Kate and Jenny prepared to leave mid-morning. They were given privacy in the living room to say their goodbyes. She heard Jenny talking with Ellie and Ben in the kitchen.

"Only eight weeks, my love," Kate whispered in his ear as they embraced.

"I know. I can hardly wait. I'll be in Mountain View in two weeks," Jack brushed her lips with his. "It's going to be hard to work today, except I know that each day is one day closer to us being together."

Kate relished the assurance of Jack's embrace. Her earlier fear from his uncertainty had vanished.

"Pastor Clary seemed glad we asked him to have a part in our ceremony," Jack said. "He looked disappointed when I told him we would get married in Mountain View, although he understood why. He's been my pastor for a long time."

"He helped me, too, when I came to Millvale. I've given him Pastor Michaels' e-mail address, so they can be in touch."

"Good." He sighed. "I guess it's time. I have to get to work, and you have to get on the road. But you'll be right here all the time," he added, pointing to his heart.

After praying together, they walked into the kitchen so he could speak to Jenny and thank Ellie and Ben.

JENNY'S CHATTER kept their trip home lively, and it helped Kate stay alert when her eyes threatened to close. They stopped for lunch at a family diner and then continued their trip.

"Thank you for bringing me, Kate. I had a great time." She paused. "May I come to visit you after you get married?"

Kate laid her hand over Jenny's. "Jack and I both want you to come."

Jenny nodded. "Do Cindy, Elizabeth, and David visit their grandparents often?"

Kate glanced at her young friend and smiled. "I think a couple of times a year."

"Oh, I just wondered." Jenny's cheeks turned pink.

Kate carefully passed the car ahead of them. "David is cute."

With a dreamy look, the teen tipped her head and pulled her hair over her shoulder. "I know," she said. "It's a long time before I should get serious about anyone, but David is a Christian."

"Do you remember the Bible study we did, and we talked about dating and relationships?"

"Yes, I do." Jenny counted off on her fingers. "I want boys who are my friends, as well as girls. I'm trying to learn more about guys in general. I've made a list of traits I'd like to have in a husband. But I want to go to college and maybe have a career. Most of all, I want what God knows is best."

"Don't ever think you know more than God, and don't try to rush ahead of Him. Jack and I weren't ready to go forward with our relationship at first. God knew when we were ready, and He brought us back together."

"How will I know if the guy is the right one?"

"Stay close to God, and don't be afraid to ask others for advice. In spite of what many teens think, it's okay to get advice from older and wiser adults. Take your time, Jenny. You'll do a lot of growing and maturing in the next few years. One of my favorite Bible passages is Proverbs 3, verses 5 and 6." Jenny joined her in saying, "Trust in the Lord with all your heart, and lean not on your own understanding; In all your ways acknowledge Him, and He shall direct your paths."

Jenny became quiet after that, and they finished their ride with only occasional conversation. She dropped Jenny off in front of the Barrows' house. At her home, she spent some time telling her parents about her weekend, and she described the cottage and the studio. Tomorrow morning she would mail the wedding invitations and start work on her wedding gift for Jack.

CHAPTER TWENTY

ate awoke, slowly becoming aware of the world around her. She rolled over and stretched, filled with contentment. This Friday, the day before her wedding, would prove to be very busy, so she took a few extra minutes to relax in bed and collect her thoughts.

She expected Ellie, Ben, Alana, and Jenny to come over right after breakfast to start working on the flowers. Ellie had ordered from a distributor close to Mountain View, getting them at wholesale prices. Kate's parents paid for the flowers, but Ellie insisted on arranging them as a gift for her friend.

"Remember, I told you a long time ago I would do this. I promised, and a promise is a promise," Ellie reminded her. "Besides, this is fun for me."

With Ellie and her team of assistants, Kate knew the arrangements would be perfect. One arrangement, however, she reserved to do herself.

"Tomorrow is the day," she whispered.

The plans she and Tim had made two-and-one-half years ago had taken on a dream-like quality. So much had happened since then. Life with its sorrow and challenges had changed her.

"God never wastes time and opportunity. Every experience in life brings change and, hopefully, growth," Pastor Michaels told her when she handed him a copy of their wedding vows earlier in the week. "You left so shattered after Tim's death, but you came back a woman that God has used to bless so many. Instead of being immobilized by what you couldn't have, you went forward with your time and talents, developing the gifts God has given you."

She had left a broken pot. God, the Master Potter, had formed those broken pieces into something new and hopefully better. All things work together for good to those who love God and wait patiently for His plans to work out, she paraphrased Romans 8:28.

Kate sat up and stretched. She and Jack both needed time to deal with the past and believe God wanted the best for them. They both needed time to grow. She believed they were ready for tomorrow.

"Tomorrow is the day I marry Jack," she whispered. Remembering she had a lot to do, she got up, showered, and dressed.

Kate and her mother reviewed their check-list of wedding details. The church ladies, following a church custom, would cater the reception. The Greenways had helped this way with other weddings in their church. Kate breathed thanks that her mother, who still tired easily, had extra help. She had been declared in remission a short time ago, but her health remained delicate. Kevin and Lindy would arrive soon, and Kate knew they would be a big help also. Her father had picked up the tuxedos on the way home from work last night. As Jack's brother and only relative, Mark had insisted on paying for the rehearsal dinner on Friday evening.

"I feel so loved and cared for," Kate confessed to Jack on the phone on Thursday night. "Everyone is pitching in to help."

"I can hardly wait for Saturday. Mark and I will be there by noon tomorrow. He has most of his things ready to move into the apartment, and the cottage is ready for us."

Kate sighed. "Maybe one day soon he'll find a special someone to marry."

"He said something that made me think he might be ready now. Maybe we inspired him."

She giggled. "Maybe. I think I'm ready."

"I love you, Katie. I know I'm ready." The confidence in his declaration made her heart soar.

Reminiscing had to be set aside when the flower truck arrived before Ellie. Kate and her parents carried the flowers inside and transformed her basement studio into a temporary florist shop.

Her paintings and artist supplies had already been transferred to Millvale, to the little studio behind the cottage. Jack and Mark would bring Jack's car, and Mark would drive back to Millvale in Kate's car, packed with her belongings. This included the painting for Jack, of the potter at his potter's wheel shaping clay into a beautiful work of art.

Both Jonathan Weeks and Mr. Lake had her new name and address in case anyone inquired after her paintings. She had had a couple of inquiries from businesses since the gallery show. And her new website, which Jack designed, had begun to open more inquiries.

Kate and her mother went over their lists, satisfied that almost everything was ready.

Kate put her arms around her mother. "Thank you so much, Mom. You and Dad have been great. I love you."

"I love you too. I am so grateful to God that I can share this time with you. I am blessed that I can see your dreams coming true." Mom pulled a tissue out of her pocket and wiped her eyes.

Kate nodded, holding her mother, not trusting her voice to say more.

The day flew by in a whirl of activity. She and Jack did not get time alone, but by the end of the day, everything was in readiness for Saturday's celebration.

Kate had one last task to perform before going to bed on the eve of her wedding. Cool air and the color and fragrance of flowers filled the basement. She looked around, appreciating all the hard work of her friends in arranging the flowers. She found what she had asked Ellie to set aside for her, and she began to work.

Two small, oval-shaped baskets stood side by side. The one held coral rose petals, the handle decorated with coral and teal ribbons, and a large bow: Melissa's flower girl basket. Beside it stood a second basket, identical but empty. Ellie had left a vase containing coral rose buds, baby's breath, and variegated trailing ivy. Carefully and lovingly Kate snipped stems and arranged the flowers in the basket, anchored by a foam block. She paused occasionally to sniff and wipe her face with the back of her hand. Finally satisfied, she picked up the basket, turned off the light, and climbed the stairs to her room. She set the basket on her dresser beside a framed portrait of Blythe.

She lifted the portrait, painted from the sketch of Blythe on that April day when they first met, or rather when Blythe first found her, as Kate stated it. She recalled that nearly perfect day and the beautiful surroundings, the day her heart opened once again to possibilities and hope. She recalled the song of the meadow, of the wind blowing through the blue spruce. She prayed that people would experience beauty and hope through her art, and that the father of the little girl would once again experience the love and joy of a family.

CHAPTER TWENTY-ONE

Kate awoke early, to the chirping of sparrows at the bird feeder and a soft breeze playing with the curtains at her open window. Her wedding day! With excitement she jumped out of bed and began her preparations for the day.

The bride and her attendants had taken their gowns to the church before the wedding rehearsal the evening before. Ellie and crew delivered the flowers to the church right after breakfast. Lindy became her mother-in-law's right-hand assistant, allowing the older woman more time to rest.

"The doctor says it will probably be a year before I gain back my strength," she confessed to her daughter and daughter-in-law. "I'm so thankful you're here to help, Lindy."

Kate knew she was spoiled and cherished by her family and friends. Her inner joy and sense of blessing expanded when her family formed a circle and prayed together before leaving for the church.

"Father in Heaven," Dad prayed, "we come before You on this day, Kate's wedding day. You have blessed us with our beautiful daughter. She has given so much of herself. Now You're blessing her with a godly man to be her husband. We've had a long journey together, Father, but You never left us. We look forward to this day and to the future. Bless Kate and Jack with many years together and use them for Your honor and glory. We thank You for our son and his family and the blessing they are. And Father, thank You so much that my dear wife is with us to share this day. In Jesus' name, amen."

"Thank you, Dad. I love you." Kate hugged each family member before she wiped away her tears and repaired her make-up.

Just before changing for the wedding, she crept into the church sanctuary to place the portrait of Blythe and the basket of roses on the front pew on the groom's side. She hoped that both Jack and Mark would be pleased with her tribute to the little girl. And she hoped Mark would accept both the portrait and the flowers as a gift.

Kate had chosen teal and coral as her colors. Her own white satin gown, and her attendants' dresses with a teal and coral swirled pattern, differed from the lacy, long-sleeved gown she had finally sold on a website. They wore simple, sleeveless A-line style dresses with shrugs. Ellie had to make a few adjustments to her dress to accommodate her changing figure.

Ellie's matron of honor bouquet differed from those of the bridesmaids by the inclusion of a large, coral rose along with rosebuds, lilies, baby's breath, and ferns. Kate carried a bouquet of coral roses, white lilies, and baby's breath, with trailing ivy. Her artist's eye appreciated Ellie's skill with arranging flowers. Melissa dropped the coral rose petals along the church aisle, one-by-one, leaving half of them in her basket.

As Kate walked down the aisle on her father's arm, overwhelming happiness bubbled up inside her. She smiled at her grandmother Greenway, who had come with Kate's aunt and uncle. Her mother's parents, unable to travel, had sent their love. Other members of her extended family sat among the guests. Mr. and Mrs. Lake sat next to Jonathan Weeks and his wife. Tim's parents and other church members smiled at her from the pews. Quite a few people from Millvale, including Mr. and Mrs. Mathews, filled in the groom's side of the church.

As they arrived at the front, her eyes connected with Mark's. He nodded and silently formed the words, "Thank you, Kate." She nodded back and then turned her full attention to Jack and the ceremony.

JACK WATCHED HER, tenderness and appreciation in his eyes. He, too, had seen Kate's gift. How could he ever deserve such a beautiful, talented, and gracious woman? "Make me deserving, Lord. Help me be the man she needs and deserves," he whispered as she came toward him. Her father kissed her and placed her hand in his. He wondered how Kate's father felt, what it would be like to give his daughter to another man. He intended to keep fully every word of his marriage vows.

Cody took his ring bearer status very seriously. He carefully held the pillow and handed the rings solemnly to the pastor at the right time during the ceremony. Later Jack would commend both niece and nephew for jobs well-done.

AFTER PHOTOGRAPHS and smiling until she thought her face might fall off, she found herself seated beside Jack in the reception hall.

Kate watched the people around her with a contented smile. Jack, seated beside her, leaned over and whispered, "What are you thinking?"

She tipped her head against his. "I'm thinking what a wonderful day this is, and what wonderful people are here. Look at them, talking, having fun. And look at us." She turned toward him and looked into his eyes.

"Yes, look at us," he whispered. "You're so beautiful today." Suddenly she heard the sound of silverware being tapped against glass. "I like this part too." He kissed her, and the tapping stopped, at least for the moment.

"Mark is doing well, don't you think?" Kate said quietly, leaning toward Jack.

She watched as Melissa stood between Mark's knees, conversing with him. Melissa had already found a place in Jack's heart, and she worked her charm on Mark as well.

Jack agreed. "He looks quite comfortable. How could he not enjoy himself, as welcoming as your family has been? You know your parents have invited him to stay with them for a few days, don't you?"

Kate nodded. "Mom asked me if I thought he would, and Dad said he would tell him he would be welcome. We all want Mark to be a part of our family." She paused and chuckled. "Actually, what Dad said was, with Kevin and Mark there, maybe they could have a checkers tournament."

"Oh, no." Jack groaned. "I have to warn my brother."

"And ruin Dad's fun? No way!"

"You're cruel. But then, I survived, so I suppose Mark will too."

"We should visit with our guests, Jack. I want to thank the volunteers who catered the reception. They did a wonderful job."

"I'm with you, Mrs. Chambers." He pulled her to her feet. "Let's mingle for a while."

As they made their way around the reception hall, stopping to speak with each guest, Kate kept repeating to herself, "Mrs. Chambers. I'm Mrs. Jack Chambers." She squeezed Jack's hand.

"Mark, Kevin, and Ben are missing," Jack said in her ear. "They've been gone for a while. I hope the car is drivable once they finish what they are doing."

"Do you want to check up on them?"

"And spoil their fun? No way."

"It was a lovely wedding, my dear," Mrs. Matthews said. "I've enjoyed getting to know your family and the people from your church. Jenny seems to be enjoying herself. My grandchildren have been asking about her."

"Jenny will probably be visiting us in Millvale, Mrs. Matthews." Kate said. "Maybe your grandchildren will be visiting you at the same time."

"We might be able to arrange that." Mrs. Matthews turned to Jack. "Now, young man, you be sure to take care of this young woman."

"I plan to, ma'am." He placed his arm around Kate. "I take my vows seriously."

"Good." Mrs. Matthews patted his cheek.

When they returned to sit at the bridal table, Kate slipped her tired feet out of her sandals. Alana and Mark sat talking quietly at one end.

Jack leaned over to whisper in Kate's ear, "What do you think?"

"I don't know. Maybe," she whispered back.

Alana looked at them over Mark's shoulder. Kate raised her eyebrows in a questioning look. Alana just smiled and turned her attention back to Mark.

Kate's mother approached them. "I think it's time to cut the cake. Although it seems a crime to cut such a beautiful work of art."

Kate had not regretted her decision to ask Sam's wife, Cathy, to make the cake. Heart-shaped tiers featured white icing in lacy patterns, topped with coral roses.

Jack's hand steadied hers as they cut the first slice. Her eyes locked with his as she placed a piece in his mouth. He tenderly wiped a crumb from her lips. Lindy took over cutting the rest and directing her children in distributing pieces of cake to the guests.

A short time later, Kate examined the group of single women who gathered to catch her bouquet. Noticing Jenny's hopeful expression, she looked at Alana and a few of the others then turned and tossed the bouquet over her head. Kate turned back around in time to see Jenny jump to reach for the bouquet, but it landed in Alana's outstretched hands. Jenny's crestfallen expression brightened when Alana turned to her and said, "Jenny, I wonder if you would take care of this for me. I can't take it with me, and I don't have a good place to store it." Jenny's face glowed as she took the bouquet from Alanna's outstretched hands.

Kate found a moment to thank Alana for her kindness to the teen. "I felt sorry when Jenny couldn't be a bridesmaid the first time. Losing her brother hurt her terribly, and she was disappointed that she couldn't wear her gown and be a part of her brother's wedding. She and I have become very close. We've adopted each other as sisters. So, having the bouquet is important to her."

"I understand," Alana said. "Besides, I can't take it with me."

"Maybe you don't really need it anyway, Lanie." Kate tilted her head toward Mark.

Alana shrugged and smiled. "Maybe. We'll have to see. Mark and I have known each other for a long time."

"I think it's time to get ready to go. Let's change and see if we can sneak out without fanfare," Jack whispered to her as her friend walked away.

Kate grinned. "You know better, my love." He twisted his mouth and nodded in a way that reminded her of Blythe. She touched the corner of his mouth, and he caught her hand and kissed it.

~

AFTER CHANGING and saying goodbyes to the family, they ran out to Jack's car amid cheers, flashing cameras and cell phones, and bubbles. With the clang and bouncing of the string of cans tied to the bumper, the thud of balloons against the sides of the car, and well-wishes of wedding guests, Jack finally pulled out of the parking lot. Kate breathed a sigh of relief and sat back in the seat.

Jack glanced at Kate. He smiled. "Happy, sweetheart?"

She turned her face toward him, her husband. "Very." She watched him as he carefully maneuvered through traffic and out to the highway. "How about you? Are you happy?"

He entwined the fingers of his right hand with her left hand. "From the tip of my toes to the top of my head," he assured her. "I keep thinking about Jeremiah 29:11. 'I know the thoughts I think toward you, says the Lord, thoughts of peace, and not of evil, to give you a future and a hope.' God had plans for Judah, then in captivity in Babylon, giving them hope for the future. God has given me hope for my future after I wasted so much time being captive to anger and lack of trust. A year ago marrying you seemed improbable, if not impossible, but God put hope in my heart, and here we are."

He turned the car into a pull-off at the side of the highway. "I think we'd better collect the noise-makers. I'll get the cans, you get the balloons. We'll put them in back on the floor for now."

In a few minutes they continued on their way.

Kate sighed with contentment as she leaned closer to him to rest her head against his shoulder. She murmured, "Speaking of the future, Jack, you never told me where we're going for our honeymoon." They had agreed it would be his responsibility to choose and plan their trip. He told her to pack casual, with one or two dressy outfits.

His face glowed with excitement. "I thought you'd like a new experience, to give you new inspiration for your painting. I want you to see the sun rise over the ocean and watch the surf pound the rocks. We can even build a sand castle, if you want. Before my parents died, they used to take Mark and me to the seashore every summer."

His eyes turned from the road to her several times as he waited for her response.

She should have guessed he would choose the seashore. "I remember seeing the pictures in the photo album. I could tell those were special times for you. I went to a lot of places with my family, and we used to go to the lakes in the summer, but the seashore will be a new experience. I always wanted to see the ocean and build sandcastles."

His face broke into a grin. "Good. Mark came a couple of times with Rachael and Blythe, but this is my first time since our parents died. We won't be able to swim now, but we can spend time on the beach. Since tourist season is over, we'll be mostly alone, together." He waggled his eyebrows.

Kate laughed and closed her eyes. "The ocean. I can imagine the sun sparkling on the sea and the sand, the waves rolling in and splashing on the rocks, and the two of us together in the glow of the setting sun." She leaned her head against his shoulder. "An artist's paradise."

Jack's voice broke into her daydream. "Do you ever wonder what we'll be doing ten or fifteen years from now?"

Kate sat up. "A home of our own, four kids, and maybe a dog. But we just got married, Jack. Let's take one day at a time."

"I know. But now that I've taken care of past issues, I can see so many possibilities for the future." He took her hand and held it to his cheek. "I have you, and we can work together."

She savored his touch. "I know from experience that life doesn't always offer beautiful sunsets and sandcastles, but we can dream."

"And face any challenges together," Jack added.

She stroked his cheek with her fingertips. "We are together, my love."

THANK YOU

To the many faculty members at the Montrose Christian Writers Conference, who have shared their expertise to teach me what it means to write well.

To my fellow writers and friends who have encouraged and inspired me through their words and prayers to continue writing.

To Kathy Cretsinger for allowing me to become a member of the Mantle Rock family and for her patience in helping me learn how to prepare a manuscript for publication. To Kathy, Erin Howard, and Pam Harris for their corrections and suggestions that helped make *Meadow_Song_* more professional and reader-friendly.

To Jim Hart from the Hartline agency, for accepting me as a client and finding a publisher for my book.

Katie McGowan left her parents and their faith behind years ago. However, when faced with a devastating betrayal, Katie is ready to go back to Carbondale, Illinois to help her elderly parents despite their tempestuous relationship. Drained by the constant friction, Katie finds emotional support and encouragement in Austin. His practical, simple faith speaks to Katie, and she finds herself yearning for a new connection to God. As their friendship grows, so does the attraction between Katie and Austin. Before her fledgling faith and thoughts of romance have a chance to take root, Katie's cheating fiancé returns, remorseful and promising change. Can her tentative faith strengthen their past love? And if her heart breaks again, will Katie's journey to faith end before it has really begun?

Faith's Journey by Heather Greer.

Mary Wade Kimball's soft spot for animals leads to a hostage situation when she spots a briar-entangled kitten in front of an abandoned house. Beaten, bound, and gagged, Mary Wade loses hope for escape. Discovering the kidnapped woman ratchets the complications for undercover agent Brett Davis. Weighing the difference of ruining his three months' investigation against the woman's safety, Brett forsakes his mission and helps her escape the bent-on-revenge brutes following behind. When Mary Wade's safety is threatened once more, Brett rescues her again. This time, her personal safety isn't the only thing in jeopardy. Her heart is endangered as well.

Rescued Hearts by Hope Tyler Dougherty.

~

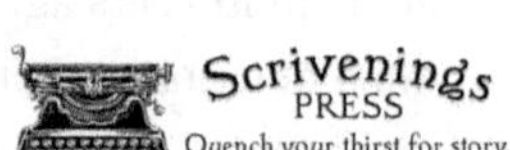

Stay up-to-date on your favorite books and authors with our free e-newsletters.

ScriveningsPress.com